Kerry County Library
Hospital Library Service

Ross dragged his mouth from hers and gazed down at her, his eyes incredibly blue.

'You'll be so good for them,' he murmured huskily. 'You're just the person they need. Well done.'

Right then, Jenna didn't feel that it had been well done. This job was what she'd worked for; it was what she'd thought she wanted. But instead of feeling any joy in her prize she felt like weeping, and she wanted to cry out that she wanted it, yes, but what she wanted most of all was him.

Why didn't he need her? Why couldn't she be part of his life?

When **Joanna Neil** discovered Mills & Boon®, her life-long addiction to reading crystallised into an exciting new career writing medical romances. Her characters are probably the outcome of her varied lifestyle, which includes working as a clerk, typist, nurse and infant teacher. She enjoys dressmaking and cooking at her Leicestershire home. Her family includes a husband, son and daughter, an exuberant yellow Labrador and two slightly crazed cockatiels.

Recent titles by the same author:

DIVIDED LOYALTIES
THIS TIME FOREVER

PRACTISING PARTNERS

BY
JOANNA NEIL

MILLS & BOON®

First published in Great Britain 2001
Harlequin Mills & Boon Limited,
Eton House, 18-24 Paradise Road, Richmond, Surrey TW9 1SR

© Joanna Neil 2001

ISBN 0 263 16962 6

Set in Times Roman 10½ on 12 pt.
07-0101-48262

Printed and bound in Great Britain
by Antony Rowe Ltd, Chippenham, Wiltshire

CHAPTER ONE

'WILL you not wait for young Dr Buchanan to get back from his home visits, Jenna? I'm sure he would want to say hello.'

Jenna shook her head. 'I don't think so, Mairi. Anyway, I expect he's going to be busy.' She wasn't at all sure that she was ready to meet up with Ross just yet, but she didn't expect Mairi to understand that. Mairi had been the receptionist here ever since Ross had joined the practice, and she thought the world of him.

Mairi's grey eyes were troubled, her fingers moving in a restless, fluttery gesture. 'But I'm sure he would want to stop and have a chat for a while— you're almost like family, and he and your father worked so well together. He's been gone for more than a couple of hours now, and he shouldn't be very much longer. There weren't too many patients on his list this afternoon.'

'Even so...' Jenna said softly. 'I had it in mind to go up to MacInnes Bluff right away, while there's still something left of the afternoon.'

'But you've only just stepped off the ferry,' Mairi objected. 'What's the rush? You can hardly have had time to catch your breath.'

Jenna gave a wry grimace. 'I suppose I'm too worked up about being back here to want to wait around. I'm late enough as it is, and there are things

I need to sort out before nightfall. I thought the crossing would settle me down and give me a chance to prepare myself for coming home, but it didn't work out that way—as soon as I saw the island in the distance, I could feel myself getting more and more emotional. I've been away on the mainland for such a long while… I hadn't realised how much I missed this place.'

Jenna smiled, recalling how she'd felt when she'd stood on the deck of the ferry, looking out over the sea, with the wind in her hair, lifting the cloudy mass of curls from around her shoulders. Even though her homecoming was tinged with sadness, she'd found herself yearning for the moment when she could step onto the quay and escape to the craggy, heather-clad hills of her childhood.

Mairi's expression softened with understanding. 'I was expecting you this morning, but when you didn't arrive Dr Buchanan said not to worry—you were never very good at timekeeping, and you'd probably turn up on the afternoon ferry.' She gave a lopsided smile, but Jenna winced at the comment.

Wasn't that just the kind of response she might have expected from Ross? He'd always watched her with a faintly guarded eye, as though he'd never quite known what bizarre situations she'd been going to get herself into, and he probably believed she was as scatterbrained as ever. Most likely he still thought of her as Robert MacInnes's carefree daughter, a reckless teenager who went around with her head in the clouds.

She wasn't a young girl any more, though, and sooner or later she would manage to show him that she was thoroughly efficient and sensible when she needed to be, and quite capable of keeping out of trouble these days.

It would have to be later, though, judging by the way her nerves were jumping. Even the mere mention of his name had the effect of throwing her defences into overdrive.

'Some problems cropped up,' she murmured, 'and I had to stay in Perth overnight—nothing I could have foreseen.'

'Well, you're here now, anyway. I just don't like to think of you going off like this straight away without out a hot meal inside you, or even a sandwich. I'm sure we could rustle something up for you.'

'I'll manage just fine, honestly. I'd sooner be doing something, keeping myself busy. The last time I was here I was in such a daze that I didn't really take in anything that was going on around me. This has been my first real sight of the island in months, and I'm desperate to get the feel of it under my feet again. If you'll let me have the keys to the cottage, I can go and look the place over once more.'

'Are you sure you don't want company, though?' Mairi persisted, a worried line edging its way into her brow. 'There are bound to be some things that are difficult for you to cope with now that your father's gone.' Her voice broke suddenly, and she went on in a choked whisper, 'Dr MacInnes was such a lovely man... We all miss him so...'

Jenna quickly reached out to cover Mairi's hand with her own. 'I know how you feel,' she said quietly. 'He had so many good friends, and his death came as an awful shock to everyone.' She paused, swallow-

ing against the lump that swelled in her throat, and
bent her head momentarily so that the silken fall of
dark, honey-gold hair shielded her bleak expression.
Then she recovered herself, taking in a deep breath,
and added softly, 'But you mustn't worry about me.
I shall be all right, I promise. I was always happy up
at the cottage when my grandparents used to live
there, and I just want to go and see it again.'

She could see that Mairi still wasn't convinced.
'The place will be cold and damp, I should think,'
her friend said fretfully. 'Your father was so busy at
the surgery he didn't have time to go up there very
often and keep it shipshape. There's no telling what
work needs to be done there now.'

'Well, at least I'll be able to see for myself and
find out the worst. Anyway, it's a bright, sunny afternoon still, and the walk will do me good.'

'There's that, I suppose,' Mairi conceded. 'You've
no need to put up with busy streets and city traffic
out here...there are just the hills and the lochs and
country fresh air.' She looked at Jenna searchingly.
'You could do with some colour in your cheeks.'

Reluctantly, she handed over the keys to the cottage, and Jenna bent to retrieve her luggage. Mairi
watched, frowning, and then asked in disbelief, 'Are
you not going to leave that lot here?'

'I don't think so. I might as well keep it with me.'
Jenna's mouth twitched. 'I've all sorts of bits and
pieces crammed in the pockets of my bags, and I'm
sure to need something if I leave any of them behind.
And, you know, my medical bag goes everywhere
with me.'

Mairi gave up trying to persuade her. 'I can see

there's no stopping you,' she muttered. 'You were always one to know your own mind.'

Jenna smiled gently as she took her leave of her friend. Outside, the sun was lowering in the western sky, casting a golden glow on the cluster of houses that made up the little hamlet nestled into the valley. She put up a hand to shield her green eyes from its glare, and slowly looked around. The calmness of the scene was soothing, and she let her gaze wander for a while over the neat homes with their well-tended gardens.

The surgery was stone-built, like the rest of the houses, but it was larger than most to accommodate the living quarters alongside the consulting rooms. Jenna stood for a while, her glance lingering on its familiar lines, on the ivy-covered walls and the timbered porch that disappeared beneath the wayward sprawl of a blush pink rambling rose. The flowering shrubs, which her father had once lovingly tended, still flourished, overgrown now and slightly ragged, in need of pruning.

She turned away, her eyes misting, and looked towards the backdrop of green hills and woodland, where a well-worn track wound its way upward. A twenty-minute walk, or thereabouts, and she would reach the crofter's cottage which had once been her grandparents' home.

Mairi had said she knew her own mind, and that was true enough. She wanted, more than anything, to make her way to the little house on the crest of the hill, and she headed that way now, moving off at a vigorous pace.

Some fifteen minutes later she had covered about

three-quarters of the distance, and she was beginning to wonder how she could have forgotten what a steep climb it was up here. With baggage to slow her down, every step was becoming a huge effort. Tomorrow she would definitely need to sort out some form of transport.

Rounding a bend in the road, she let her luggage slide to the ground and stood to catch her breath and take in the view. Her heart lifted as her gaze lingered on the tranquil loch where her father had once fished on his weekend breaks from the demands of the surgery. It was fed by a small stream that started higher up in the hills and flowed intermittently, depending on snow melt and rain, and after a long wet spell a gentle waterfall carried the overflow from the loch down in a tortuous path towards the sea.

Just now, a solitary figure stood by the water's edge, reeling in a fishing line, his back to her. She watched him for a moment, then gathered up her bags ready to set off once more. He was preparing to cast out again, but he must have heard her movements, or the scattering of gravel underfoot, because he turned around and she recognised him at once. Fortyish, and greying a little around the temples, he worked a small croft to the west of the island.

She waved, and called out to him. 'Hello, Donald. Have you caught anything today?'

He sent her a beaming smile. 'Is it you, Jenna? Now there's a sight for—' His words ended on a sharp note as his fishing line swung towards him in a wild whiplash movement and became tangled up in something, and the next moment Jenna saw him clap a hand to his face.

'What is it, Donald? What's happened?' Abandoning her bags, she hurried over to him, concerned that he might have hurt himself badly.

'The hook must have caught me,' he muttered. 'Drat the thing. What have I done, can you see?'

'Move your hand, then I might be able to get a better look,' she ordered, frowning, and when he did as she'd asked, she could see that the hook was embedded in his flesh.

'The hook has caught in your eyebrow,' she told him, tentatively trying to dislodge the metal without causing him any more pain. 'No, it's gone right in— it isn't going to move that easily.' She studied him briefly. 'Are you OK?'

He nodded and grimaced. 'Do you think you can get it out for me?'

'I'll try. I won't be able to pull it out the way it went in, because the barb will tear your skin. The best thing will be to push it through the way it's headed.'

He winced. 'You do what you think best. I'd do it myself, but I can't see without a mirror. I'm sorry to be such a nuisance, Jenna.'

'You're hardly that,' she murmured. 'It's my fault because I came along and shattered your concentration. Here, come and sit over by the tree for a minute or two while I go and get my medical bag. I can give you something to anaesthetise it while I pull it through.' Gently she nudged him down, and went to retrieve her bag from the grassy verge at the side of the track.

'You're a real gem,' Donald murmured when she set to work a minute or two later, injecting the area with a local anaesthetic. 'I always knew you'd make a fine doctor one day. We were all sad when you went away, but I knew you'd do well for yourself. Your father used to keep us up to date with how you were doing, you know. He was so proud of you.'

'I really didn't have any choice but to follow his example,' she answered softly. 'I couldn't let him down, now, could I?' Taking care not to cause any more damage, she snipped off the line, carefully pushed the hook through the tender ridge of his eyebrow and slid it free. Then she handed him the offending object. 'There you go,' she murmured. 'I'll just clean the skin again with antiseptic and you'll be as good as new. Well, almost.'

'Thanks, Jenna.' He fingered his brow lightly when she'd finished, and asked, 'Are you on your way up to the cottage?'

'That's right, I am. It's been a while since I saw it last, so I thought I'd pay a visit.'

'Looks like you'll have company up there,' he commented with an odd quirk to his mouth, and she stared at him, mystified, until she saw that he was looking beyond her, and she heard the sound of a vehicle rounding the bend in the road. It was slowing down.

Jenna turned to watch as the car drew to a halt by the roadside, and she waited while the driver switched off the engine. A prickling sensation started at the back of her head and slowly travelled down the length of her spine.

The car was different from the one she remembered—this was a gleaming silver hatchback—but the profile of the man at the wheel was one she would never forget.

His features were carved into her memory—strong bones, a firm jaw, an attractively formed, sensual mouth that made her knees go weak just for looking. Ross Buchanan had been part of her childhood, an essential part of her growing up, and she didn't doubt that his image would remain with her for ever.

He was getting out of the car now, unfolding his long body from the driver's seat and swinging the door shut. His movements were easy and supple, his body lithe. He had that quality of always being calm and confident, no matter what chaos reigned all around, and maybe that was what made his patients so loyal to him.

He didn't come over to them straight away. Instead, he stood for a long moment, simply looking across the expanse of heath that separated them, and even from this distance she could feel the intensity of that dark gaze. Her breath caught in her throat as he started to move towards her.

'Hello, Jenna,' he said, and the deep, smooth sound of his voice made her feel warm inside, reminding her of rich, dark chocolate. 'It's good to see you again. Mairi told me you were on your way up here. She was worried about you going off on a nostalgia trip.'

His blue glance slanted over her, his eyes widening a little as his gaze shifted from her shoulder-length hair with its mass of springy, natural curls to flick down over her slender figure. She was wearing jeans and a soft cashmere jumper that clung to every curve, and his lingering, searingly intimate scrutiny left her feeling tingly all over. Her reaction troubled her. He still had that way of looking at her that made her feel

hot and dizzy, and she still didn't know how to deal
with her response to him.

'She had no need to be worried. I told her I'd be
fine.' Her voice was husky to her own ears, but she
was thankful she managed to keep it on an even note.

His mouth tilted at the corners. 'Well, you know
Mairi. She can be like a mother hen at times.'

Donald coughed, and Ross turned to look at the
fisherman. 'Hello, there, Donald. What have you been
doing to yourself? Your eyebrow's red and swollen.
Have you been in a fight?'

'You could say that.' Donald gave a wry grin. 'I
had a bit of an argument with a fish hook and Jenna
came along and acted as referee—but if anyone else
asks I'll say I had a battle with one that got away.'

Ross's mouth twitched. 'Lucky for you that she
came on the scene when she did.' His gaze shifted to
the medical bag which lay open on the grassy bank,
and Jenna bent to pack away the things she had used,
thankful for something to keep her occupied.

Conscious of him watching her, she hoped that her
sudden nervousness didn't show. She was feeling
quite shaky all at once, and that bothered her, but it
had been a shock, seeing him like this, even though
she might have guessed that he would come after her
sooner or later. She'd been hoping for later.

Ross hadn't changed a bit. His dark grey suit was
immaculate, the jacket sitting well on his broad shoulders. He was lean but muscular and flat-stomached,
and his legs were long and powerful. He was still
sinfully good-looking, she acknowledged warily, with
his black hair close-cropped, lending him a devilish
appearance. In fact, everything about him sent out

warning signals that had all her senses swinging cha-
otically to instant alert.

'What happened to your car?' he asked, as she
closed her bag and stood up to face him once more.
'Didn't you bring it over with you on the ferry?'

Jenna shook her head. 'I left it behind in a garage
in Perth. A new head gasket, the man said. But then
he started talking about skimming something or other,
and maybe the engine was on its way out...and, to
be honest, after that he started losing me a bit.
Anyway, it all comes down to probably costing me a
small fortune, so I thought I'd sort something out
while I'm over here instead.'

His eyes glinted, his mouth making a wry shape.
'You're lucky that car lasted you as long as it did. I
seem to remember warning you, before you bought
it, that there were too many miles on the clock, but
you'd already made up your mind it had your name
written on it.'

'It was a lovely little car,' she told him firmly. 'It
just got a bit tired and run down, that's all.'

He laughed and then hastily tried to turn it into a
cough as she glared at him.

'I'll give you a lift up to the cottage,' he said.

'I don't want to put you out. I'm sure you must be
busy.'

'It's no trouble,' he murmured easily. 'I can manage an hour before evening surgery.'

His blue eyes narrowed as he looked across to the
roadside where she had dropped her luggage. 'You
must have found it hard going, dragging that lot all
the way up here. I can't begin to imagine why you

felt the need to do that—it would have been perfectly
safe back at the surgery, you know.'

She nodded. 'I do know that, but I wanted to keep
it with me.'

He shrugged, powerful shoulders moving beneath
his jacket. 'I'll go and load it into the car.'

She thought of the steep climb that remained, and
wilted, saying gratefully, 'Thanks.'

With a tilt of his head to Donald, he went to collect
her bags and hoist them into the boot, leaving her to
bring her medical case and a light holdall which she
lifted and slung over her shoulder. She turned back
to Donald.

'Will you be all right now?'

'Of course. It's good to see you back on the island,
Jenna. I expect I'll see you around the village, will
I?'

'I'm sure you will. Look after yourself.'

Ross was waiting by the car, and she went over to
join him a moment later.

'Mairi said you were out on your rounds,' she commented as he held the door open for her to slide into
the passenger seat. 'You must be finding things difficult to manage on your own now that my father has
gone.'

'I've had time to adjust,' he said, seeing her settled
and going around to the driver's seat and starting the
engine. 'The early days were difficult because his
stroke came out of the blue and none of us could take
in what had happened at first. Everything was chaotic
for a while, as you can imagine, but we had to keep
going, and at least I've been able to get some locum
help.' He glanced at her obliquely. 'How are you cop-

ing? We didn't get much of a chance to talk at the funeral, but you seemed to be bearing up.'

Her shoulders hunched briefly. 'It's been hard at times. Some days are worse than others—days when I ask myself why it had to happen to him when he always seemed so fit and healthy—but at least I've had my work to keep me from dwelling on things too much.'

'He might have had a weakness in the blood vessels for most of his life, and without knowing that the problem existed there was very little anyone could have done to prevent the stroke from happening. And then he pushed himself to give his best to his patients. He always worked above and beyond what was strictly necessary. He should have had a partner long before I came on the scene.'

She nodded. 'He always cared so much about everyone, and treated his patients like friends. I'm glad you were there to share his workload.' She was silent for a moment, remembering how pleased her father had been to welcome Ross to the practice. 'I suppose now you'll be looking to take on another doctor?'

'It's all in hand. Someone's due to start in a couple of months, but she has to finish a stint up in Inverness first.' He concentrated for a moment on a bend in the road, then asked, 'How are things with you? Last I heard, you were still at that large health centre in Perth. Are you on leave now?'

'Yes, I am. I haven't had a holiday for some time. The practice has been so busy, and the rotas had to be juggled constantly. People were off sick over Christmas and New Year, so I filled in then, too. But now I have to take the time off that's owing to me or lose it altogether, so it turns out that I have several weeks free.'

'Are you here to sort out your father's effects? There must be a lot of loose ends that need tying up.'

Jenna nodded. 'I suppose I'll have to get my mind round to it. Things have reached a point where I can't really put it off any longer.'

They had reached the top of the hill by now, where the ground began to level off. Sheep grazed on the meadowland, enclosed by a rough stone wall, and further to the west the slopes were covered by trees that provided shelter from the winds that could occasionally sweep over the island. Jenna leaned forward in her seat, eagerly watching for sight of the little settlement where her grandparents had lived.

'There it is,' she breathed, as the white-painted house came into view. It was just as she recalled it from her last visit, though it had been neglected somewhat, with climbing plants spreading untidily over the walls, and the windows were lost in a scramble of greenery. She smiled fondly at the dormer bedroom, peeping out from under the thatched roof, where she'd sometimes slept as a child.

Ross stopped the car, and they climbed out and went over to the cottage together. The house wasn't totally isolated as there were three other cottages scattered at intervals over the fields, but it stood proudly, overlooking the sweep of a broad bay. If you listened carefully, you could sometimes hear the waves crashing on the shore when the tide was coming in.

'It must be a couple of years since I last came up here,' she said. 'I didn't always get the chance to visit it when I came to see my father. We were often busy doing other things, but it was always there, in the back of my mind. Has it been empty the whole time, do you know?'

'For the most part, except for the occasional week-end when your father might have stayed there. Robert sometimes thought about renting it out as a holiday cottage, but it would have taken a lot of work to make it ready and he didn't get round to doing anything about it. There were always too many other demands on his time, especially in the tourist season when the surgeries were at their busiest.'

'He told me he was considering renovating it. At least my grandparents had the foresight to have a wa-ter supply and electricity connected.' She frowned, momentarily deep in thought. 'I suppose letting it out to people would take care of the summer months at any rate. I'm not sure anyone would want to come up here in the depths of winter, though. They might think it's too isolated.'

'That's what happens when you live in the city,' Ross murmured dryly. 'You get too used to the com-fort of central heating, and supermarkets just a short distance away. Not to mention the attractions of the night life.'

'Well, you certainly wouldn't find much of that around here.' She turned the key in the lock and pushed open the door. A damp, faintly musty smell met them, and she wrinkled her nose a little. 'The place needs airing,' she murmured.

She walked through the hall to the kitchen and cast a glance over the furniture in the room. There was a pine dresser displaying beautifully decorated china crockery, and a serviceable table and chairs, good, solid furniture that still looked in reasonable condition, and she could imagine the room as it had once been, with cheerful curtains at the windows and shining copper pans on the shelves. All at once she smiled up at Ross, remembering the happy times she'd spent here with her parents and grandparents.

'I used to love coming here in the holidays or at weekends,' she told him. 'The stove would be lit and the kitchen was always warm and friendly, and Nan would have spent the day baking. We all sat round the table, and Nan would bring out the bread, still warm from the oven, and a big fruit cake, and Grandad would produce a ham and carve thick slices for all of us.'

She glanced over at the old wood-burning stove that stood in a corner of the room. 'The cooker's gone now—it was past its prime—and Dad brought in a tabletop hotplate a couple of years ago so that he could heat up the odd tin of soup if felt like it. He would come up here if he needed a break from the surgery. He used to go to the lake to fish, and then he liked to come back to the cottage to read the papers for an hour or so.'

Her vision blurred briefly, and she swallowed hard, before saying, 'Perhaps I could get a fire going in the sitting room, and maybe the stove will warm the kitchen up if I can get it to light.' She looked down at the box that used to hold wood for the fire and saw that it was empty. 'I expect there are some logs in the outhouse—I'll go and have a look.'

Ross sent her a thoughtful glance. 'I'll do that for

you,' he murmured. 'You stay here and have a look around.'

Perhaps he recognised that she needed time to get her emotions under control and wanted to give her some space—whatever his reasons, she was grateful for his consideration.

When he'd gone, she stood for a moment in quiet contemplation, before getting herself together and going to the sitting room. The furniture had been carefully covered with dust-sheets, and she wondered who had done that. Ross, probably.

The old fireplace, with its iron grate, was clean but empty of tinder, and she tried to imagine how it would be with a fire burning in the hearth. She remembered how her grandparents had occasionally stood a kettle on the trivet to heat over the fire, and how they'd made toast of a winter evening.

She went back into the kitchen and searched in the cupboards until she found an old kettle that was still serviceable. Taking it over to the sink, she filled it with water, then set it to heat up on the hot plate while she went to fetch crockery from the pine dresser.

Ross came back as she was rinsing china mugs. 'Most of the wood is damp,' he said with a grimace. 'The outhouse roof has sprung a leak, but I managed to find a few bits that might burn—enough to get you started, at least.'

He filled the wood box, then set to work, loading the stove and trying to get a flame going. 'There,' he said after a while, standing back to survey his efforts. 'That seems to have done the trick.'

Jenna came and stood beside him, feeling warmed already by the golden glow. 'It's amazing what a difference a bit of heat can make, isn't it? It makes me think how the house might be restored to the way it once was, bright and warm and homely. Once I get the fire going in the sitting room, it'll be even more like old times.'

His smile was gentle, but tinged with something like caution. 'I know this place means a lot to you, Jenna,' he said softly, 'and I can see why you would want to spend some time here, reminiscing, but I think you'd be better leaving the sitting-room fire until tomorrow, when you've more time to sort things out. If you get a fire going in there tonight, and the chimney's blocked and you're not here to deal with it, you could end up with more problems than you counted on.'

She frowned. 'But I shall be here.'

He was on his way to the sink to rinse his hands, but he stopped momentarily to send her a disbelieving look. She added defensively, 'Why wouldn't I be? And I need to get the fire going so that it will heat the back boiler, and then I can have hot water.'

'What do you mean, you'll be here?' He was frowning now. 'You'll be staying at the surgery tonight, won't you? There'll be ample time to sort this place out tomorrow.' He washed and rinsed his hands in cold water and looked around for a cloth to dry his hands.

She shook her head, rummaging in a drawer and bringing out a clean hand towel. 'I don't think so,' she said, passing it to him. 'I've made up my mind to stay here while I'm on leave. I might as well since the place is empty—it seems the most sensible solution.'

His dark brows shot upwards. 'How do you work that one out? There's no food in the cupboards, the rooms are cold and damp, and I can't imagine why you are even thinking about staying here when your father's house is there, waiting for you. You could be warm and comfortable at home, instead of being miserable here.'

'But there is food. I brought one or two bits with me—tea, milk and a loaf of bread, butter and cheese—so I won't starve.' She foraged in her hold-all. 'And cookies, see? So I can at least offer you tea and biscuits.' She grinned at him, but he sent her a dark scowl in return.

'I'm serious about this,' he said. 'I don't see why you're even considering staying here.'

'Because I want to. Because it's mine, and it's familiar to me, and I feel as though I belong here.' Determinedly, she ignored the gathering fierceness of his expression, collecting up wood from the box and taking it through to the sitting room.

Ross followed her. 'There's no sense in that. You can stay at the surgery.'

'I can hardly do that, now, can I?' she said in a reasonable tone. 'Not when you're living there.' She placed the logs in the grate, along with crumpled newspaper she'd found in one of the cupboards, and tried to get a blaze going.

'What difference does that make, for heaven's sake? It's your home, your father's house, it's always been your home.'

'But it isn't now, not any more. The surgery belongs to the practice, so I only really have a part-share in the place. That's one of the things we must

24 PRACTISING PARTNERS

sort out while I'm here—we must get everything fin-
alised properly along the lines the solicitor suggested.
I'm sorry I've left it so late; I just never got around
to signing the papers.'

'The papers are irrelevant,' he remarked brusquely.
'You can stay in your old room whenever you want,
just as you did when your father was alive.'

'That's the point, though, isn't it? When he was
alive, things were different. Can't you imagine what
people would say if the two of us were to live together
under the same roof?'

'Why should they say anything? They know you're
here for a short stay, and it's perfectly reasonable for
you to want to stay in your father's house.'

'You're wrong. You know, as well as I do, that this
is a small community, that people gossip, and you, of
all people, have a reputation to keep up. You're their
doctor, you have to be above reproach.'

His mouth twisted in that expression of cynicism
she remembered so well. 'If you're so concerned
about what people will think, I'll move out—I'll go
and stay with my mother.'

'You can't do that.' She wasn't having him put
himself out on her account. 'It's not as though she
lives on this island and it would mean a boat ride
over here every day. That's far too much hassle. You
need to be at the surgery, and I won't hear of you
moving out. And, anyway, there's absolutely no need
when I have this place. I'm here now, and I'm staying
here, no matter what you say.'

His blue glance shimmered over her in a flash of
impatience. 'You're not thinking straight, Jenna. You
can't be, if you're planning to stay here in the cold

and damp and risk your health. I've a good mind to bundle you into my car and take you home with me right now, and that would be an end to it.'

'But you won't,' she said calmly. 'After all, I'm not fifteen years old any more, and, you must know that I could kick up one hell of a fuss if you stop me doing what I feel to be right. You wouldn't like that, believe me.'

His eyes narrowed on her, suddenly dark as a storm-tossed sea. 'You haven't changed a bit, have you, even after all this time? You're too stubborn for your own good, do you know that?'

'Just as long as we understand each other,' she answered him, smiling sweetly. 'Now, I think I can hear the kettle whistling—a cup of tea would go down well, don't you think? We've both had a busy day.'

'Don't imagine you can change the subject so easily,' Ross muttered thickly. 'You were always headstrong, and it always got you into difficulties that you couldn't handle. You may not be fifteen any more, but it seems to me that you still need to think a little longer before you act. I care about what happens to you, Jenna, you've been like part of my family since you were three or four years old, and I don't feel inclined to stand idly by and watch you head for trouble.'

'Did you ever?' she muttered dryly. Nothing had changed, had it? He was as protective as ever, determined to make sure that she came to no harm, in spite of herself, and that might have been a good thing, an endearing way to go on, except that she'd moved beyond that.

She'd grown into womanhood, but he still thought

of her now in the same way that he'd always done, as though she were a rebellious young girl he needed to watch over...a sister, almost. And, oh, how that rankled!

CHAPTER TWO

IT RAINED in the night, and when Jenna went into the bathroom in the morning she found that the ceiling and walls were damp and there was a fusty smell about the place. Yesterday, when she'd seen that the paint was peeling off the walls in places, she'd supposed it was because of the steamy atmosphere in the room over the years, but now she wasn't so sure. Ross had already said that the outhouse roof was leaking and that made her wonder whether there might be a problem with the main roof as well.

It was too much to dwell on with an empty stomach, and what she needed to do before anything else was to go and stock up with provisions. She would go for a walk across the bay to the village store and maybe that would help her to get her priorities sorted.

After a quick breakfast of tea and toast, she took the steps down to the beach and walked along the seashore. It was a crisp, bright morning, and she breathed in the fresh air, letting her eyes feast on the glorious sweep of the bay. There were some fishing boats out on the water, but they were too far away for her to be able to see the occupants. To the west the rugged cliffs made a home for seabirds and gave way to a rocky shoreline, but here was all white sand and gentle waves that rolled in and foamed gently on the shore.

She listened to the sound of the gulls calling to

27

each other as they circled overhead, searching for food, and smiled. Being by the sea made her feel so much more energised and revitalised.

She missed so much of this, living and working in Perth. She loved her job as a GP—it was the culmination of years of effort, studying and working long hours—but she was glad of this chance to take time out. It was so beautiful here, peaceful and restorative, and she hadn't realised how much she'd needed a change of scene until now.

At the far side of the bay, she took the sloping path to the main street of the village, where Aisleen Jamieson's shop stood next door to the post office. Aisleen was just a few years older than Jenna, thirty to Jenna's twenty-six, and they'd been friends since as far back as she could remember.

'You're staying up at the cottage, then?' Aisleen said. 'Are you going to be all right? Ross said it needs some work doing on it if it's to be comfortable to live in.'

'He thinks I'm mad to want to stay there,' Jenna said with a wry smile, 'but it will only be for a few weeks.' The alternative he'd offered, staying with him at the surgery, even for just a short time, wasn't one she could begin to consider. She was far too aware of him, and his simply being around made her feel restless, unsettled, and stirred up all sorts of feelings in her which she'd hoped would stay buried. 'It is a bit damp, but at least the weather's improving every day so that will help.'

'Have you thought about what you'll do with the cottage when you go back to Perth? Will you sell it?'

'I don't know, yet,' Jenna answered. 'It's one option, or I could maybe let it out to summer visitors. That's what my father was thinking of doing. Either way, there's such a lot needs doing to the property to bring it back to anything like the way it once was, and I'll need to give it some thought.'

'At any rate, it looks as though you're going to be busy over the next few weeks,' Aisleen said, as she packed detergent and soap powder and dishcloths into carrier bags, alongside groceries. 'From the amount of stuff in here you could be planning a blitz.'

'Something like that.' Jenna laughed. 'What doesn't move gets washed. When that's done, I might have a bit more of an idea what the next stage is, but I expect a coat of paint would brighten things up.'

'It's a good thing you're fit and healthy.' Aisleen smiled. 'The very thought of spring-cleaning or decorating makes me wilt.'

'I should think it would. You've enough to do, looking after a couple of young children and trying to keep this place going. Are you coping all right? A couple of years back you were having some problems with your diabetes. Is that all under control now?'

'Och, yes. Ross sorted out the insulin dose for me, and I manage the injections myself well enough. As long as I stick to the diet he gave me, I'm fine.'

'I'm glad, and you're certainly looking well. You must come over to the cottage some time soon and we'll have a meal together.'

'I'll do that. I'll look forward to it.'

A customer came into the shop then, and Jenna said a quick goodbye and made her way back to the house in a cheerful frame of mind. Now that the sun was shining the roof didn't seem to be quite so much of

a problem, and she could at least take a look at it and
see what the damage was.

There was a ladder in one of the outhouses, she
recalled, and when she'd stowed away her groceries
in the kitchen cupboards she hauled it out and
propped it up against the side of the house.

She'd never been too good with heights, and it
didn't help that the ladder wobbled precariously as
she gingerly climbed up, making her stomach lurch
queasily. The wooden rungs creaked and she had the
horrible sensation that they were giving a little beneath her feet as she strained to get a better view. It
was probably just nervous tension that made her think
that way, and as she teetered at roof level she dug her
fingers into the thatch to steady herself.

'What on earth do you think you're doing up there?
Have you lost your senses? That ladder should have
been condemned years ago, from the look of it.'

She recognised that voice instantly, and could
hardly miss the impatient, incredulous note that
threaded the words. Ross must have arrived when she
was in the outhouse—that would be the reason she
hadn't heard his car pull up.

She turned to look down at him, and caught a fleet-
ing glimpse of his grim expression, but the movement
intensified the creaking and started her swaying all
over again, and for a moment she was much too shaky
to give him any kind of answer. Instead, she mumbled
something incoherently into the thatch and concentrated on getting her nerves back together again.

'Jenna?' He was waiting, and she could tell from
the sharp way he spoke her name that if she didn't

say something soon he was more than likely to come
up the ladder after her and fetch her down physically.

She gritted her teeth and muttered tersely, 'There's
a hole somewhere, a leak. I'm trying to find out how
big it is.'

'Get a roofer in to see to it,' he said in a caustic
tone. 'You look about as secure up there as a butterfly
in a force-ten gale. Come down, now, before you fall
down. Just ease yourself back—I'll hold the ladder
still.'

She swept a quick glance over the roof once more,
and caught a glimpse of a couple of gaps in the thatch.
Grimacing, she turned away. One of them was much
bigger than she'd bargained for, and she wondered
bleakly whether she would need to have the whole
lot renewed or whether it could be patched.

At least she'd managed to see for herself what the
problem was, and she consoled herself with that
thought as she cautiously felt her way back down the
ladder.

Going up had been a lot easier than coming down,
though, and now, as she tested each rung with the
ball of her foot, she had the uneasy feeling that the
whole apparatus was about to come apart at the
seams.

Glancing carefully over her shoulder, she saw
Ross's tall frame outlined darkly against the sun, and
she stared, the image of long, lean masculinity holding her spellbound for an instant. No one should look
that good, that disturbingly male.

He was wearing a beautifully cut suit, and as he
moved towards her she had an overwhelming impres-
sion of rugged strength, long, tautly muscled legs and

powerful shoulders. He was stunning, there was no other word for it. Just looking at him would be enough to send any woman's blood pressure sky-high.

'Keep going,' he urged forcefully. 'You're quite safe...I'm not going to let you fall.' He reached for her, his jaw set at a firm angle, his glittering blue gaze narrowing on her in a way that was distinctly un-nerving, so that her heart rhythm skidded, then swerved into a new and faltering tempo. 'You're al-together too reckless to be left to your own devices,' he said in a taut undertone. 'I don't know what you were thinking of.'

Jenna pulled in a deep breath. She wasn't going to let him make her feel that she was in the wrong. Definitely not.

'I shall be fine,' she said. 'I know what I'm doing. You worry too much.' Why should she feel any qualm of dismay just because he disapproved of her actions? He didn't like it that she'd made up her mind to stay here, at the cottage, and now he thought she shouldn't be checking out her own roof. What would be the next thing?

She braced herself to deal with him, annoyed with herself for letting him put her at such a disadvantage. What she really needed to do was to let him know that she was a wholly independent woman, perfectly capable of looking after her own affairs, and the best way to do that was to show him that she was totally calm and unruffled and in complete possession of her-self.

Just then, though, her foot slipped as one of the lower rungs gave way, and she made an unexpectedly sudden descent, slithering the rest of the way down the ladder and completely losing her balance.

Ross's strong hands shot out and caught her around the waist, effectively breaking her fall, and she collapsed against him, the breath leaving her body in a small explosive gasp.

'It's all right...I have you.' His arms went around her, holding her securely, and a flush of heat suffused her entire body as the softness of her curves was crushed against his hard length. Her fingertips tangled with strong biceps and fluttered nervously as she encountered the ripple of firm muscle, the tightening of sinews.

Jenna blinked, staring up at him in sudden confusion. 'I, uh, I'm not sure what happened just then,' she said thickly, biting her lip. 'My foot slipped somehow... I didn't expect to come down quite so fast...'

He stared down at her. After all his heated comments of a few moments ago, he wasn't saying anything at all now, not one word, and somehow that bothered her more than if he'd poured a torrent of recriminations down on her head. Instead, he was simply very still, unusually still, looking down at her bemused features with an oddly arrested expression, his powerful body braced with tension as he held her steady. She wished she could know what he was thinking.

Then a muscle flicked in his jaw, sparks of flame flared into life in his dark eyes, and she had the uncomfortable feeling that whatever was on his mind it could only spell more trouble. His fingers curved around her arms, gripping her firmly.

'You were lucky you didn't break something,' he said in a roughened tone. 'Look at the state of that ladder—it should have been thrown out years ago. No wonder it fell apart when you stepped on it. What induced you to take a risk like that? Are you totally reckless? Don't you have any sense at all?'

'But I thought it would… I mean, it was—'

'No—don't bother trying to come up with an answer.' His mouth slanted with derision as he released her, putting her away from him at arm's length. 'You never did know the meaning of the word caution, did you? That's why you and my brother were forever getting yourselves into situations you couldn't handle.' He sent her a hard stare, his blue gaze lancing into her with all the power of a laser, so that she almost flinched.

'This was just an accident,' she threw back at him. 'I don't know why you're making such a big thing of it. My foot slipped, that's all. I'm not a young girl any more who can't look after herself. You don't need to concern yourself over anything I do.'

'If that's true, then I'm very glad to hear it,' Ross said tersely, 'because there's no way I want to lose sleep over what trouble you might be getting yourself into. I had enough of that to last me a lifetime when I fished you out of the loch.'

A wave of hot colour flooded her cheeks. How could he bring that up, after all this time? She'd been a child then, thinking only what an adventure it would be to go sailing on a makeshift raft with Alex, Ross's brother. She'd been a reasonable swimmer, but the thought that the stunt they'd planned might have been a dangerous one had never occurred to her—or to

Alex, for that matter—and how would she have known that she would fall in the water and become entangled in the weeds and vegetation that flourished in the loch?

They'd tried to keep their mission a secret, guessing that their parents might put a stop to it. Ross, though, eight years older than she was, and in the habit of looking out for his young brother, must have had wind of what they'd been about because he'd suddenly arrived at the loch. She'd heard him call out to them sharply from the shore, but it had only been much later that she'd realised how shocked he must have been by what he'd seen.

Submerged and choking in that bitterly cold water, she'd remembered little afterwards about the way Ross had rescued them, but she knew from what Alex had said later that he'd tried to move heaven and earth to drag them to safety. She could believe it. Ross had always been tough and strong, and she'd never known him give up on anything.

Jenna vaguely recalled his desperate efforts to pump the water from her lungs, and the way he'd tried to keep her warm until the ambulance came, wrapping his jacket around her and holding her close.

To this day, it made her go hot all over to think of the way she'd clung to him, sobbing with relief and trembling from the sheer terror of what had happened. She'd been terribly afraid for Alex, and had begged Ross to make sure that he was all right.

Ross had comforted her, coaxing her to be calm, but later, when they'd been released from hospital, he'd been angry with both of them, frighteningly angry, so that she'd hardly dared put a foot wrong for weeks afterwards.

And now here he was, dragging the whole thing up again. 'I'm hardly going to get myself into that sort of situation nowadays, am I?' she said tightly, and scowled at him when he lifted a cynical dark brow. 'And anyway,' she added tersely, 'the ladder looked perfectly safe to me at the time...' Frowning, she tossed a glance towards the offending object, then studied it a little more carefully. 'Though I can see now that it might have been a bit splintered here and there, and maybe looks a little...' she grimaced, peering closely at the broken rungs '...the worse for wear.'

'"Rotten" is probably the word you were looking for,' he said with a rasp. 'And broken beyond repair would be a much better description.'

'Well, yes, it is broken,' Jenna admitted grudgingly. 'Of course, I can see that it isn't safe *now*— but anyone could have made the same mistake that I did. And the main thing is I'm fine, nothing bad happened, and I'm sure that if you hadn't come along when you did I'd have managed to sort things out well enough.'

She paused and sent him a thoughtful glance. 'Why are you here, anyway? Have you finished morning surgery?'

'Surgery finished an hour ago,' Ross said briskly. 'I'm actually in the middle of doing my home visits, but my mother asked me to stop by here, as it's on my way, to pass on an invitation. She wants to know if you'd like to have lunch with her today. Of course, she knows that it's short notice and you might have other things to do.'

'That was thoughtful of her.' Jenna smiled, thinking of Flora Buchanan and her kindness over the years. Since Jenna's mother had died in a climbing accident long ago, Flora had stepped in and watched over her like a mother hen. 'I'd like that. I'm not too busy here...' She pulled a face. 'At least, there's nothing that can't be put off until later, and I was thinking of going to see Flora some time this week. I just didn't want to land myself on her without some forewarning.'

'She's always happy to see you. I'll give her a ring and let her know that she can expect us. Shall I pick you up in about an hour? I've another visit to make over at the Sinclairs' house, but as soon as I've finished there I'm off for lunch and I can come back for you.'

'The Sinclairs live over by the jetty, don't they?' When he nodded, she went on, 'So it would be easier all round if I came with you, wouldn't it? Otherwise you'll be doubling back on yourself.'

'That's true enough. It would make things simpler, if you don't mind doing that.' He looked around and frowned at the ladder. 'Have you finished everything you need to do around here?'

She nodded. 'There really isn't much more I can do about the roof just now. I'll need to talk to someone about the extent of the damage, and find out what it will take to repair it.'

His dark brows slanted at a rakish angle. 'Now she sees sense!'

Jenna sent him a withering stare, and went to put

the ladder away, but he forestalled her. 'I'll do that. You go and lock up, or do whatever you need to do, and we'll be on our way.'

She joined him in his car a few minutes later, having quickly changed into a skirt and sweater, and he drove them to the Sinclairs' house.

Jenna would have stayed in the car while Ross went to see his patient, but Shona Sinclair, a pretty young woman with dark, wayward hair and harassed features, saw her and gestured to her to come into the house. 'Come in, Jenna, won't you? It's good to see you again.'

She led them through the hallway to the sitting room. 'It's my boy, Ewen, Dr Buchanan. He's not been well these last few days, very listless and out of sorts, and now he has a rash and a bit of a cough. I didn't want to risk taking him over to the surgery in case it made him more poorly, and I wondered if he might pass on the infection to any newborn babies there. I've heard these things can cause problems in very young infants, and I didn't want to turn up on a day when you had the babies in for immunisations.'

'That's all right, I understand. I'll have a look at him, shall I?' Ross went over to the settee, where the child lay back on cushions, half-asleep but paying a passing interest in a video. He squirmed miserably as Ross approached, struggling to scratch an irritation on the back of his neck.

'Can I see?' Ross asked gently, and a few minutes later, when he'd examined the child, he said, 'Poor lad, you're covered with spots, aren't you? But try not to scratch, Ewen. You'll make yourself sore and even more uncomfortable if you do that.'

Ewen was about four years old, and Jenna could see that the red, blistery rash extended behind his ears and over his trunk and limbs. No wonder he was feeling sorry for himself.

'It's chickenpox, Shona,' Ross said. 'It's not usually a problem with children—adults are the ones who suffer most if they get it. But he does have a chest infection as well, so that's probably making him feel worse. I'll write out a prescription for some antibiotic medicine. He's a little bit feverish, so you could give him some children's paracetamol to bring his temperature down, and if you dab a bit of calamine lotion on the spots that should relieve the itchiness. It's important that he doesn't scratch, because that might cause scarring, or an infection might set in.'

'I'll keep an eye on things,' Shona said. 'I thought it might be chickenpox. Some of his friends went down with it a few weeks ago. Perhaps I'll give his dad a ring and ask him to go over to the pharmacy in his lunch-break. He'll be back in a while.' She turned to Jenna. 'I heard you were coming back here, Jenna. Are you here to stay this time, or is this just a flying visit?'

'It's just a short stay,' Jenna told her. 'I had a couple of weeks at the coast to wind down with friends, and now I'm here to sort out all my father's loose ends, if I can.'

'That'll take some time, won't it? Well, it's good to see you back here, anyway.'

They left a few minutes later, after chatting about old times for a while, and then Ross drove to the jetty, where his boat was moored.

It was a small motor boat, a cabin cruiser, essential

for his work because the practice covered this island and the two smaller neighbouring islands. It wasn't always easy for the more elderly people to make the trek to the surgery if they were ill, and the same applied to mothers with young children. Ross held surgeries once a week on the neighbouring islands, but he and her father had always made home visits where necessary.

Mrs Buchanan had always lived across the short stretch of water, but Jenna had been a visitor to the Buchanans' farm from when she could barely toddle. Her father had taken her with him sometimes when he'd had to see patients, and her mother had often gone over there to spend time with friends.

The crossing took only a few minutes, and Jenna sat back and enjoyed the ride as the boat sped over the water.

'How is your mother?' she asked a few minutes later as Ross cut the engine and manoeuvred the boat alongside the quay.

'Actually, she's a bit frail these days,' he said with a frown. 'She's had one or two falls, and ended up with some nasty bruises.'

Troubled, Jenna said quietly, 'That must be worrying for you.'

'It is,' he admitted. 'She lives on her own in that big house, and I can never be quite sure that she's all right. The last time she fell, she broke her hip and lay on the floor for about an hour before a neighbour found her and called me.'

She gave a small gasp. 'Ross, that's dreadful.' She laid a hand gently on his arm. 'What happened? Has she recovered all right from it?'

Ross nodded, his hand going over hers in brief acknowledgement. 'I took her to hospital, and they were able to operate on her within a few hours. She walks a little stiffly sometimes nowadays, but apart from that she seems to have got over it well enough. The trouble is, her bones are more fragile now because she suffers from osteoporosis, and she won't consider hormone replacement therapy, which might help.'

'Why won't she do that?'

He helped her from the boat, and she stood on the quay, watching as he secured the boat. 'I think she's uncertain about the long-term effects of hormone therapy. She thinks it isn't natural—she's always been a believer in home-spun remedies, a good diet and plenty of exercise and fresh air, but, of course, some people are more prone to loss of bone density than others.'

'She was ill a few years ago, and had some prolonged treatment with corticosteroids, didn't she? That won't have helped her bones at all.' Jenna was silent for a moment as they set off along the road towards his mother's home. 'There must be something you can do to put your mind at ease,' she said at last. 'Can't you arrange something with the phone company? They have systems for alarm calls, don't they?'

'I've made sure that she has a phone with an alert button so that she can always reach me and her neighbours in case of an accident, but it still doesn't put my mind totally at rest. I don't suppose anything will. Even if I went to live with her, I'm out so much during the daytime and I'm often on call at night.'

'Could I do anything to help while I'm here? I can

give her my mobile number, and I could be on hand if she needs me.'

He smiled. 'Thanks, Jenna. I know you would help, and you can try, but my mother is such an independent soul I don't think she would accept unless she was in dire need.'

By this time they'd arrived at the farm where Flora Buchanan had lived for most of her adult life. It was so different now from when Ross's father had once cultivated the land and sheep had roamed on the hillsides. Nowadays it was more of a smallholding. The house, though, was as familiar as ever, solidly built of stone and decked with ivy and flowering shrubs which gave it a warm and friendly appearance.

'Hello, there—come in, both of you.' Flora met them at the door and gave Jenna a hug before she waved them through to the kitchen. The smell of good home cooking filled the room and made Jenna's mouth water in anticipation.

'It smells wonderful in here,' she said appreciatively.

'I've made a hotpot for all of us,' Flora said, setting out plates and busying herself at the oven. 'I didn't think you'd have had time to do any cooking for yourself, so I've made a chicken and mushroom pie as well for you to take home with you—and a fruit cake. They should keep you going for a while.'

'You must have been at work for hours to do all that,' Jenna said, her eyes widening appreciatively. 'Is there anything I can do to help?' she added quickly, but Flora shook her head and sent her over to the dining table.

'You sit yourself down there with Ross,' she said.

'I know he has to get back to the surgery for the afternoon list, so the sooner you eat the better. If I didn't feed him, I don't know when he'd stop for a proper meal.' Her eyes skimmed Jenna's slender shape, and she added, 'You look as though you could do with a few good dinners inside you, too, my girl. You're another one who must have been working too hard.'

Jenna laughed. 'You always spoiled me, Flora. You know how I love your hotpots and your home-made cakes. If you hadn't invited me over here, I'd have been around anyway in the next day or so—not just for the food, of course!'

'You're welcome here any time, hen. How is your job going? Is it what you wanted?'

She nodded. 'The people are really nice, Flora. It's a big practice, a health centre with more than half a dozen doctors working there, and they're building a massive extension so that they can offer more facilities.'

'What sort of facilities?' Ross asked, passing the casserole dish to Jenna so that she could help herself to the appetising meat and vegetables.

'An obstetric wing mainly, but there will be a paediatric clinic as well, and a unit for welfare supplies. It was almost finished when I went on leave, so by the time I go back there will be just the finishing touches to be added.'

Ross studied her carefully. 'Are they looking for people to work in the clinics, or are the posts already filled?'

'Some vacancies have been filled already, but

they've been interviewing for the main posts—doctors to run the clinics, mostly.'

'Are you applying? It sounds like what you've always wanted. You've specialised in paediatrics, so you must have a strong interest.'

She nodded. 'It would be the ideal promotion, wouldn't it? A brand new unit, and a community I'm already familiar with. I've been for an interview, but I shan't know the result for a while. Eventually, of course, I would like to try for a partnership.'

'It's what your father would have wanted for you,' Flora said. 'He was really keen for you to study on the mainland and get the best qualifications you could. He knew there wasn't much work here. A lot of folk hereabouts either commute from the mainland or have part-time work alongside their smallholdings or the fishing. But you'll do fine over there as a paediatric doctor. You were always very good with children.'

Jenna smiled doubtfully. 'I haven't got the job yet, Flora, and the competition was very stiff, from what I heard. They might find someone else far more suitable than me.'

'Never. You'll be well in the running. They'd be fools to overlook you, my girl. Tell her, Ross. You know how hard she's worked.'

'She doesn't need me to tell her.' Ross's mouth made a wry shape. 'We spent hours going through old exam questions, and she wouldn't rest until she had it right. She was ambitious as a young girl, always knowing what she wanted and determined to get it.'

'My dad wanted me to get the best qualifications I

could,' Jenna admitted. 'He said I should spread my wings and find out what was out there on the mainland.'

'A darned sight more than there is here, I'll be bound.' Flora scanned the table. 'Eat up. There's more in the dish, and I don't want to be throwing away good food.'

Jenna helped herself to more vegetables and said thoughtfully, 'Were these grown on the farm?' When Flora nodded, she asked, 'How do you manage everything? It must be difficult for you to cope here on your own.'

'A couple of part-time workers come and help out with the crops, or I would be in trouble. The rest I can do by myself. There are a few hens for the eggs, and there's the herb garden to see to, and then, of course, I have my painting. I still sell the occasional water colour in the shop in the village.'

Jenna smiled. 'They're very good. Especially the landscapes. You did one of the cottage, didn't you? My father had it on the wall in his surgery.'

'It's still there,' Ross said. 'You must come up to the house and sort through all the things that belonged to him.'

'I suppose I should.' The thought made her feel bleak and empty inside. It was such a final thing to do. It meant that things must change, that she ought to move on, and something inside stopped her from wanting to do that.

Flora broke the momentary silence that had fallen. 'How are you getting on at the cottage? Ross tells me it's damp and draughty, and you're likely to catch your death from pneumonia up there.'

'Or from falling off ladders,' Ross put in under his breath.

Jenna sent him a scorching glance.

'I shall be fine,' she told Flora, who was looking concerned. 'Take no notice of him. I'll keep the fires burning for a day or so to warm the place up, and eventually I'm planning to do a bit of decorating to get it looking homely and fresh again. I'll have to sort out a few things first, though. The roof needs repairing, and the kitchen needs modernising...and I thought I might have a new boiler installed.'

Ross sent her a quizzical glance. 'That's a lot of expense to go to. Are you thinking of selling the house?'

'I haven't made up my mind yet and, anyway, I can't really do anything with it until it's been renovated. I thought I might ring round and get a few quotes before I decide to go ahead with anything.'

He nodded. 'That sounds like a good idea.'

There was a knock at the door, and Flora said, 'That will be James, come for some eggs. He brings his little granddaughter with him when he can. She likes to go and gather the eggs for herself.'

She went to the door and opened it to a man who looked to be in his sixties, grey-haired and stocky-framed, his skin weathered by years spent out in the open. Another fisherman, Jenna thought.

'Here you are, Kirsty,' Flora acknowledged the little girl who appeared at his side. 'You take this basket and go and get the eggs.' Wide-eyed, the child took the basket and went off excitedly, her dark curls dancing as she ran. Jenna didn't think she could have been much older than Ewen, about four years old at the most, and she was slender, like a little ballet dancer.

'Come in, James,' Flora said. 'There's tea in the pot.'

'I thought I might have timed it about right,' James said with a slow grin. He nodded to Ross and Jenna, and Jenna thought there was a stiffness about his movements, as though he was in some pain.

'How are you?' Ross said, and James sat down at the table with a faint grimace.

'Shouldn't complain, I suppose. The old rheumatics play up from time to time, you know, and my head hurts these days something wicked. I wonder if you might take a look, seeing as how you're here.'

'You probably overdid the drink last night,' Ross said amiably enough. 'I saw you going into the tavern at eight and then again when you were rolling out at closing time.'

James grinned. 'One of life's little pleasures. Where would I be without a drop of the hard stuff from time to time?'

'Headache-free, most likely,' Ross murmured, smiling. 'Come on through to the sitting room and I'll have a look at you.'

The two men went off into the other room, and Flora said with an exasperated sigh, 'That's the trouble with having friends as patients. He never gets a minute without he's having to work. Folk don't think of it like that, though. They see him, and they think, ah, he'll sort it for them, save them having to go to the surgery. And he never says no. He's too soft by far. He's already been up half the night on call, and he still has a full day's work to do.'

Jenna frowned. 'I thought he said he has a locum helping out?'

'Is that what he told you?' Flora's mouth twisted scornfully. 'From time to time, maybe. It's always difficult to get staff to work out here in the wilds, and the summer's on us now so there's more demand from other surgeries for locums while doctors are on holiday. And, of course, this is just the time when Ross's workload increases because of all the tourists who come over here.'

'I hadn't realised that he was so overloaded,' Jenna said quietly. 'He didn't say anything to me about being out on call last night.'

'He wouldn't,' Flora said. 'It's not his way.'

There was a tapping on the door then, and little Kirsty appeared with her basket of eggs. 'Look at these,' she said happily, showing them off. 'There's lots. Mummy will be pleased—she might do strangled eggs for our tea tonight.'

Flora and Jenna both chuckled. 'Might she now, bairn? That's very good. You'll grow big and strong on those.'

Ross came back into the kitchen with James, and Jenna saw that the older man was clutching a prescription. He looked over the eggs in the basket and told Kirsty she'd done a grand job. After a minute or two they said their goodbyes and promised to call again the next week.

'I shall have to be getting back to the surgery,' Ross said, shrugging his shoulders carefully to ease his taut sinews, and Jenna watched the ripple of muscle with absorbed fascination as he reached for his jacket. 'Thanks for the lunch, Mum. I'll stop by again tomorrow. Will you be OK? You've everything you need?'

'I'll be just fine,' Flora said. 'Don't you worry about me. And, anyway, Alex will be coming home soon for the holidays, you know.'

'So he will. He said something about studying for his exams, didn't he?'

'Aye, and so he ought. It's all very well to be good at the practical stuff, but he won't be able to get a decent job as a vet without his exams.'

'I dare say there's time enough yet.' Ross turned to Jenna. 'Shall we go, then? I'll take you over to the surgery, if you like, and you can pick up your father's four-wheel drive from there. It's been kept under cover in the garage these last few months, but I've had it serviced for you so it should be in tip-top condition.'

Jenna blinked. 'I'd forgotten all about that.'

'I thought you might have. I mentioned it to you last time you were here, but you weren't really taking much in back then.'

'No. I suppose I wasn't. This time around, I'll try to pay more attention.'

She turned to his mother. 'Thanks for that wonderful lunch, Flora. I'll come over and see you again soon. You take care of yourself.' She kissed her on the cheek, and went out with Ross, taking the path to the jetty.

'I'm stuffed after that big meal,' Jenna said with a smile. 'Your mother has always been good to me. She has a heart as big as a house.'

'She has that. She thinks of you as one of her own, you know.'

Jenna nodded. 'She's worried that you've been working too hard,' she said as they walked along. 'Why didn't you tell me that you've been struggling on your own? There's no need for you to do that while I'm here. You know I'd be willing to help out with the surgeries.'

He frowned. 'She shouldn't have said anything. I'm managing just fine...and you certainly will not help out. You're on leave. Enjoy your time on the island.'

'How can I do that,' she asked softly, 'when you're working day and night, risking your health and worrying your mother?'

'I'll pacify my mother. You don't need to do a thing. You're here to relax and get your energy back before you go home to Perth, not to take on more work.'

'I'm not offering to work full time,' she said. 'Just to fill in for you when you need a break, to act as a locum for when you're expected to be in two places at once. The money will come in handy, too, for the renovations. Besides,' she murmured, 'I don't believe you actually have a choice. Have you given any thought to the alternative?'

He looked at her with deep scepticism. 'What alternative would that be?'

'It's obvious, isn't it? If I'm not helping you, just think of the time I'll have on my hands. There will certainly be time enough for me to have a go at the roof by myself. I remember, years ago, my grandfather showing me how he put the thatch in place. It didn't look too difficult, and it would be a lot cheaper than getting someone in to do it.'

His gaze narrowed sharply on her. 'You wouldn't dare.'

'Wouldn't I?' Dancing light flickered in the depths of her green eyes as she watched the doubt creep into his own. 'How can you be sure? You, of all people, must know how hard I find it to resist a challenge.'

CHAPTER THREE

'I'M NOT going to let you do this, Jenna,' Ross said,
when they were back at the surgery and she'd insisted
on telling Mairi that she would act as his locum.
Frowning, he drew her into the coffee-lounge, away
from Mairi's inquisitive gaze. 'Why would you want
to help out when you're on holiday? You need to take
a break, or you'll make yourself ill.'

'And the same doesn't apply to you? I've had a
couple of weeks by the coast with friends, enough to
build up my reserves again. And I don't see why I
shouldn't put in a few hours a day here, where I know
most of the people and I can be of some use. It isn't
as though I'll be thrown in at the deep end, not knowing my way around. Besides,' she added on a thoughtful note, 'I meant what I said about the money. If I'm
going to make improvements to the cottage, it will
take some cash, probably a lot more than I have at
the moment, so any extra will come in handy.'

Ross frowned, looking at her with a trace of doubt
in his eyes. 'If cash is the problem, I could loan you
some. I know it will be a while before your father's
estate is settled, but there's no need for you to struggle in the meantime. You can always come to me if
you need anything.'

She shook her head, but smiled up at him. 'You're
really sweet to say that, but I don't want to have to
rely on anyone to sort things out for me. If I've

52

learned anything these last few years, it's that I like to try and manage things for myself. And if you'd only let me help out here, it could work out well for both of us.'

Jenna studied him, trying to gauge the impact of her words on him. 'We could draw up a rota for the next few weeks so that one or other of us is on call. That way, we might both be able to have some free time.'

He was still frowning, and she couldn't help noticing the dark shadows of tiredness around his eyes. Why wouldn't he accept what she was offering? He'd been out on an emergency during the night, and had worked throughout the day, so it was no wonder that he was looking thoroughly weary.

She gently touched his arm. 'Why don't you go and get some rest?' she murmured softly. 'I can take this afternoon's surgery for you, and be on call tonight.'

'No, I won't let you do that,' Ross said firmly, and it sounded so final that her heart sank at his stubbornness.

'But I—'

'We'll talk about it again some other time,' he cut in shortly.

She made a face. 'I shan't change my mind, if that's what you're thinking.'

His mouth curved in a brief smile. 'We'll see about that. Anyway, let's go and sort out this four-wheel drive of yours.'

He was dismissing the subject, and she accepted it with good enough grace for the moment. Perhaps he'd forgotten how determined she could be.

They went out to the garage, and he unlocked her father's vehicle. She sat in the driver's seat and tried things out until he was satisfied that she was comfortable with the controls.

'I'll be OK,' she told him. 'You don't need to take me through every step, you know. I have been driving for quite a number of years.'

'I know that...but bear with me on this, will you? These can be tricky to handle until you get used to them, and I don't want you going on your way until I feel sure you're at ease with everything.'

'I promise I won't hold you responsible for anything that happens,' she said impishly. 'I can take care of myself, believe me. I'm a grown woman now, right down to my toes.'

Ross looked startled for a moment, then trailed a glance over her feminine curves, lightly skimming the soft fullness of her breasts and the smooth line of her skirt where it faithfully moulded her hips, before letting his gaze glide down to linger on the long, slender shapeliness of her legs. He made to say something, then closed his mouth and gave her a crooked grin instead.

'I can see that well enough,' he admitted finally in a husky drawl. 'It doesn't stop me from wanting to make sure that you stay safe, though. If anything, it just adds to the confusion.'

Jenna rolled her eyes upwards in defeat, and resigned herself to paying close attention to his comments about handling the vehicle. There was no way he was going to let her go until he was satisfied.

'You'll do,' he said at last, then glanced down at his watch. 'I ought to go and get ready for surgery now. Before you go, I think Mairi has some bits and pieces for you to take home—the landscape painting my mother mentioned for one, and then there are a few things that belonged to your father.'

He watched her carefully. 'Will you be all right loading them up, or do you want me to help you to do it later?'

'I'll be fine,' she murmured. 'You go and get on.'

He hesitated for a moment, then nodded and went off to see to his patients, leaving her to go and have a word with Mairi on her own.

'He could do with some help here,' Mairi said, 'no matter what he might have told you. You're just the person he needs to give him a hand. You won't let him put you off, will you?'

'I won't. You can rely on me for that. Give me a call if you need me,' she told her. 'No matter what he says, I'm here to help out.'

When she'd collected the boxes that Mairi had put to one side, she drove back to the cottage and spent the rest of the afternoon making plans for the renovations.

Over the next day or so, a man came to fix the roof thatch so that Jenna could at least rely on no more damp getting in, and she made a start on the sitting room, stripping off the wallpaper and rubbing down the paintwork. Friends dropped by, and sometimes she went with a small group of them into town to eat at one of the newer restaurants or visit the cinema.

She didn't see anything of Ross over the weekend, and found herself wondering what he might be doing.

Mairi phoned a few days later, when Jenna was

getting dressed and thinking about breakfast. 'Ross has gone out on an emergency call, to a heart patient, and it doesn't look as though he'll be back in time to take morning surgery. Normally I'd tell people he's been delayed, but I wondered if you'd be able to come over?'

'I can be there in half an hour.'

'Thanks, Jenna.'

True to her word, she was at the surgery first thing, ready to share a coffee with Mairi and look over the morning's list.

'I'm so glad you're going to be helping out,' Mairi said, her mouth curving with satisfaction. 'He would never have asked, but you're exactly what this place needs.'

'I'll do what I can,' Jenna murmured. Her eyes were wistful as she glanced around the room. Years ago, she would have leapt at the chance to work here, alongside her father, but it had never worked out that way. Ross had stepped in to fill the breach while she'd been away at medical school, and now the practice belonged to him.

He'd already said that he was bringing someone in from outside and, of course, she was glad that his problems would ultimately be resolved. She'd broken her ties with this place in the intervening years, and now she'd forged a career for herself away from the island.

A few minutes later she went and introduced herself to the occupants of the waiting room, and then made herself at home in the little room that her father had used for his surgery. It was clean and well organised, and the shelves were still decorated with the cheerful collection of ornaments of Scottish wildlife which he'd added to gradually over the years. Ross had offered to give them back to Jenna, but she'd refused, telling him that they belonged here.

Blinking away the nostalgic memories, she rang the bell for the first patient.

Sarah Mackie was a young woman in her late twenties, and it was fairly obvious that she was suffering from a sore mouth. Her jaw was a bit swollen on one side, and to add to her problems she had a bloodshot eye which was giving her some pain.

'You look a bit the worse for wear,' Jenna said with a smile. 'What have you been doing to yourself?'

'I wish I knew,' Sarah said wryly. 'I think I might have scratched my eye somehow, and that could have caused the problem. A bubble of something came up on it and burst, and now another one's started.'

'Let me check that first,' Jenna said, reaching for her ophthalmoscope and shining it into Sarah's eye. 'There may be a slight infection starting in there,' she murmured a minute or two later. 'I'll give you some antibiotic eyedrops. They should clear it up, but if you're still having trouble in a few days come back to the surgery.'

She had a look inside Sarah's mouth, and added, 'As for the jaw, it looks as though your wisdom tooth is still trying to make its presence felt. That can be quite troublesome, I'm afraid, but painkillers should help.'

Mairi brought her a cup of coffee an hour later, and said with a pleased grin, 'I knew you'd settle in just fine. I told Dr Buchanan so.'

'He's back, then?'

Mairi nodded. 'Just walked in this minute, in a hurry to make up for lost time with surgery and stunned to find you'd already made a start. Too tired to put up much of a fight, I'll be bound. I left him with a mug of coffee and a bun to make up for him missing his breakfast. He was up and about in the wee hours, seeing a patient into hospital, and now he has a string of home visits waiting.'

After chatting for a minute or two more, she slipped away back to Reception, leaving Jenna to sip her coffee and check the notes on the computer while she waited for the next patient to come in.

When the door swung open, though, it was Ross who came into the room. He quirked an expressive brow in her direction.

'You don't give up, do you?'

'Not easily.' She grinned. 'I'd have thought you'd know that by now.'

He sent her a wry smile. 'And what exactly do you have in mind, now that you're here?'

'I'll carry on with morning surgery, while you do the home visits, if you like. There have been half a dozen calls already, Mairi tells me. A couple on the list that could be bronchitis or flu from the sound of things, and then there's a sprained back and a hysterectomy patient who's just home from hospital. The district nurse thought the wound site looked a bit inflamed, and she wondered if you'd go and have a look.'

His mouth curved. 'I can see you've been getting to grips with things. That's very efficient of you. You weren't trying to forestall any objections I might have, by any chance?'

'Why should I do that? I don't expect you to have any.' She gave him a sweet smile, hoping that her wide green eyes looked entirely innocent. 'I've asked Mairi to work out a rota for us. I'd prefer to keep the afternoons free, for the most part, so that I can work on the cottage, but I'll do mornings, and I'll be available to help out in an emergency. I'd like to do the mother and baby clinics as well, if it will help.' She wasn't going to push her luck by offering to do any more just yet.

His eyes crinkled around the edges. 'I can see that I'd be wasting my breath, trying to persuade you otherwise. Thanks. I appreciate your help,' he said, giving in, and she felt a surge of relief. 'Just say if it all gets too much for you.'

'It won't.' He left her, and she smiled to herself, pleased with the way things had gone.

Some time later, when the waiting room had emptied and the patients' notes had been updated to her satisfaction, Jenna tidied her desk and went to Reception.

Mairi greeted her with a cheerful grin. 'You've finished, then? Everybody here has been telling me how glad they are to see you around again. Alex came in and I told him that you've been doing a great job.'

'Alex?' Jenna's brows lifted in surprise. 'He's been here?' Of course, Flora had said that he was coming home.

'Aye. He came in on the ferry this morning, and he asked me to say hello to you. He's away now, wandering about the village for a wee while, but I expect he'll be back by the time you've finished here.'

He would have come to see his brother, of course,

and the two of them would probably go over to Flora's house later. Jenna had always got on well with Alex, and it was good to know that he'd come home for a spell.

She placed her bundle of patients' notes in the tray on the counter ready for filing, and went to deal with the repeat prescriptions Mairi had left in her wire tray.

Alex came in a few minutes later, and clasped Jenna in a bear hug as soon as she was within reach. Like his brother, he was tall and dark-haired, though his hair was rakishly untidy and the clothes he wore were casual, jeans and a sweater.

'Put me down,' she protested, laughing, as he swung her round, lifting her up off the ground. 'Anyone would think we hadn't seen each other for an age.'

'We haven't, not for at least five weeks. It seems like an age. I missed you.' He grinned at her, his blue eyes sparkling. 'We might well live in the same city, but we don't meet up nearly enough. You work much too hard, you know. I thought now you were back home you might take a break and then we could spend some time together, but what do I find? Here you are, busy again.'

'Have you two quite finished holding onto each other?' Ross's dry tones reached them from the doorway, breaking into their laughter.

'Uh-oh.' Alex cast him a sideways glance. 'Hi, bro'. Good to see you.'

'And you.' Ross's mouth made a crooked shape. 'Are you going to let her go? This is a medical centre, not a dating agency. Anyone might walk in and wonder what's going on.'

'Spoilsport.' Alex wrinkled his nose and turned his attention back to Jenna. 'Just when I was enjoying myself.'

Ross sent him a dark scowl, his gaze slanting over their entwined bodies and coming to rest on Jenna in a way that made her feel distinctly uncomfortable. Diamond glints flashed in his blue eyes and she wondered uneasily why she was being censured.

She dug her fingertips into Alex's shoulder. 'Perhaps you'd better do as he says.'

He gave a heavy sigh. 'If I must.' Reluctantly, slowly, he released her. 'It's great to see you again, Jen. I thought I'd meet up with you sooner or later, but I didn't expect to find you here at the surgery.'

'I'm just helping out for a while.' She glanced at his luggage, over by the door. 'Are you going to stay with your mother? How long will you be over here?'

'I'm here just for two or three weeks. My old room's always there for me. Mum keeps it ready and waiting. She likes to keep an eye on me and feed me up whenever I come home.'

'So this will be a lazy fishing and beachcombing break, will it?'

'I wish.' He pulled a face. 'I'm supposed to be swotting for exams. Not exactly my idea of fun, but I suppose I'll have to get down to it some time.'

'But you like veterinary work, don't you? I thought you were settled on that. You're not planning another change of career, are you?'

'I didn't give up my science course on a whim,' Alex protested. 'I really thought I was doing the right thing choosing that to begin with, and I could go on to other things from there...but then I realised that

I'm much happier working with animals. I like the practical side of things.'

'We know that,' Ross commented dryly. 'It's just theory you have trouble with. The studying part always seems to get in the way.'

'Only because I'd rather be out and about doing things, rather than sitting at a desk in a stuffy room. It's what comes of growing up in a place like this. It spoils you for anything else.'

'Maybe.' Ross put his medical bag down on the counter and went over to the coffee percolator. 'Does anyone want a coffee?' He poured the hot liquid into the mugs that were set out on a tray, and handed one to his brother. 'I'm going over to the house for the lunch-break. Shall I give you a lift, or are you staying in the village for a while longer?'

'You can give me a lift, thanks.' Alex accepted the coffee, and sipped appreciatively. 'How is Mum? She doesn't tell me a lot when I phone.'

'She'll do. She walks a bit stiffly at times, but she's managing well enough. Annie said she'd come with me and spend a few hours with her this afternoon while I'm working. We weren't expecting you till tomorrow, so it'll be a double treat for Mum today.'

'Annie's still around, then? Still got the hots for you, has she?' Alex asked, his eyes dancing with mischief, and Jenna felt her heart plunge into freefall.

Ross sent him what should have been a quelling stare, but Alex went on irrepressibly, 'Now she's back from agricultural college, she'll be around quite a lot of the time, I expect. Should we be getting ready for a June wedding?'

'You can get ready for a wedding when I tell you,

and not before,' Ross said repressively. 'Have you finished your coffee yet? I said I'd pick Annie up at one, and it's nearly that now.'

'I'm ready.' Alex gulped down the remains of his drink and turned to Jenna. 'I'll come over to the cottage one evening soon, shall I, and maybe we could spend a night in town together?'

'I'd like that,' Jenna said, trying on a smile and hoping that none of her unhappy thoughts showed. So Annie was still on the scene, was she?

Nothing had really changed, had it? Ross and Annie had been an item when Jenna had gone off to medical school, and from the sound of it their relationship was set to hot up pretty soon.

The thought made her thoroughly miserable. What had she expected? That Annie would have found herself someone else and settled down to bring up a family? Why would she, when Ross was unattached, and still waiting for her?

She said to Ross, 'I've some tubes of paint in my bag for Flora, and some of the specially fine brushes she likes. Perhaps you could give them to her? I found them in a shop in Perth, but they were in the bottom of my case and I've only just hunted them out.'

'She'll like that. Thanks.' He smiled, his attractive mouth slanting in the way she remembered from way back. 'You've been a great help here this morning. I'm really grateful for all that you've done—and from what I heard before I went off to do the home visits, the patients are, too. Are you going to go and spend the rest of the afternoon on the beach?'

'Some of it, perhaps, but I'm having a new boiler

system installed at the cottage and I want to check on the progress so far.'

'I expect you've done wonders at the cottage already.' He gave her a quick smile. 'Make sure you get some leisure time. I'll see you tomorrow.'

Mairi cleared away the coffee-mugs when Alex and Ross had gone for lunch. 'It'll take Annie a while to find her feet, I expect. She finished her farm management course a few months ago, and she's looking for a place of her own now. It isn't easy to get the backing she needs, though, especially with her being so young.'

'It's probably more difficult for a woman to be taken seriously,' Jenna remarked. 'Annie's always been strong-minded, though. I expect she'll get what she wants in the end.' Would that include Ross?

She gathered her things together. 'I'm away now, Mairi. I'll see you in the morning.'

Jenna's days settled into a pattern of seeing patients at the surgery in the mornings and work on the cottage in the afternoons. She'd picked out new soft furnishings on a trip into town, and she was pleased with the way things were beginning to look.

Ross came by unexpectedly one evening when she was in the middle of hanging curtains in the sitting room. It had been a struggle on her own, but now he held the curtain for her while she hooked it in place.

'You've made quite a few changes here,' he said, glancing around appreciatively. 'It all looks very homely.'

She'd made covers for the settee and chairs, and had arranged soft cushions on the seats. Here and

there, on shelves and window ledges, she'd added
touches of colour with delicate vases and pretty glass-
ware that she had picked up in sales. Then she'd
brought in flowers from the garden to make a bright
display on the coffee table.

'Thanks. It will be better when the extra kitchen
units are in place and the bathroom has been tiled.
I'm doing as much of the work as I can myself, but
it all takes time. I thought I'd start on the main bedroom next.'

'I could help, if you like. Painting's easy enough,
and I can hang wallpaper.'

It was considerate of him to make the offer, but
she smiled and said, 'I think you have enough to do.'

'I wouldn't have made the suggestion if I hadn't
meant it,' Ross murmured. 'And I'm not the only one
who works hard. It seems to me that you've taken a
lot on, too. I'm impressed. You've coped brilliantly
with everything that's happened these last few
months, and now you're taking on even more chal-
lenges.'

'It helps to have people around who show that they
care,' she admitted, 'and I've been lucky that way.'

She made coffee for them and they drank it in the
sitting room by the window, which looked out over
the fields to the woodland beyond. The light was beginning to fade, and it was getting harder to distinguish the various features of the landscape. She asked,
'Have you finished work for the day?'

'Fingers crossed. I've just made the last house call,
and thought I'd stop by on my way home and see
how you were getting on.'

Ross glanced around. 'I meant what I said, you

know. I'll give you a hand with the decorating...at the weekend, perhaps. And one day soon, if it's fine, we might spend some time by the sea. We could take a picnic, if you want.' He smiled. 'It will give you a bit of a break at least. You've been spending such a lot of what should be your holiday time hard at work and I feel guilty about that because I'm at the root of it.'

'You don't need to feel guilty. Like you, I wouldn't have offered if I hadn't wanted to do it, and if I'm hard at work it's only because I want to get the house looking right.'

'Even so, it would be good to spend some time just relaxing, don't you think? The weather's been a bit bleak these past few days, but the weekend might be fine enough to be out and about.'

Jenna smiled. 'I think I'd like that.' It would be good to spend the day with him. No strings, no involvement. And he was only suggesting it because he felt she'd been under pressure to work at the surgery. But it would be good just to be close to him for a while, away from any stresses and strains. He looked as though he could do with getting away from the cares of the surgery.

His mobile phone started to bleep and he acknowledged it with a sigh.

'Dr Buchanan,' he said into the mouthpiece, and then listened carefully, a frown etching itself more deeply into his brow as he concentrated on the voice at the other end of the line.

'I haven't seen or heard anything,' he murmured. 'I'm up at MacInnes Bluff. I'll look around the area and see if there's any sign of her. I'll get back to you if I find anything.'

He cut the call, and Jenna looked at his worried face with concern. 'What is it? What's wrong?'

'Little Kirsty Blake has gone missing,' Ross said abruptly, getting to his feet in one lithe movement and walking briskly towards the door.

'She went with her brother to Brae Farm,' he went on. 'He helps out there for an hour or so each day, and she must have wandered off while he was distracted for a moment. She's been gone for two or three hours now and the police are searching for her. They think she can't have gone far, but they're looking in a two- or three-mile radius of the farm. That includes this area. I'm going to help with the search.'

Jenna recalled the little girl who had gone to Flora's farm for eggs. She was barely four years old.

She hurried after him. 'I'm coming with you,' she said, grabbing her jacket from its hook. 'We should take torches with us—it's getting dark out there already. And maybe a blanket. We don't know how well protected she is against the cold.' Her mind was ticking off possibilities, the need for speed vying with practicalities.

'Good idea. Sergeant Harris says she's wearing pale blue dungarees with a white T-shirt underneath. Light colours, so they should show up better than most.'

Jenna threw some things into a holdall, reached for a couple of torches from the kitchen cupboard and grabbed her medical bag as an afterthought. They hurried out into the evening air. It was grey outside on the hills, the sombre cloud cover heavy with the threat of rain.

'We'll do better on foot to begin with,' Ross said. 'She might be huddled down somewhere and we might miss her if we keep to the road.'

Jenna nodded and fastened the zip of her jacket, already feeling the chill of the cold wind. She was terribly fearful for the little girl who might be wandering, lost and afraid, in the hills. Anything might have happened. If she'd gone into the woodland over to the west, she could be trailing about for hours, not knowing the way out, and she might be frightened by the sounds of the forest as night fell. The child's family must be worried sick.

'Ought we to split up to look for her?' Jenna couldn't think where to begin. Her heart was racing, the worry of increasing darkness weighing heavily on her.

'We should stay together, I think. Two pairs of eyes will be better than one. You might see something that I miss. We'll check the undergrowth as we go, and look down by the burn.'

God forbid that the child had fallen into the water. Jenna bit her lip, shining her torch so that the beam of light focussed on every rise and hollow.

From time to time, she called out, 'Kirsty, sweetheart, where are you? It's Jenna and Dr Buchanan. Shout if you can hear me.' They stopped and listened for any sound that might be carried on the air, but heard only the eerie whistling of the wind and the rustle of leaves.

Together, she and Ross trekked over the meadow grass for nearly an hour, searching copses where the moonlight filtered through the trees and cast long shadows over the ground, but they found nothing.

Ross used his mobile to check how the police search was going, but there was still no news of the little girl. Jenna's mouth trembled as the gravity of the situation pressed down on her. She shone the torch around and moved forward over the uneven ground with increasingly desperate steps. Then her ankle twisted and she lost her balance and stumbled heavily into Ross. His arm shot out to steady her.

'I'm sorry,' she gasped. 'I must have caught my foot in a rabbit hole.' She shivered in the cold wind, feeling miserable with growing frustration, and felt tears spike her lashes. She brushed the back of her hand over her cheeks to dash the dampness away.

Ross drew her close, warming her, his arm firm around her shoulders. 'Did you hurt yourself? Let me take a look.'

'No…I'm all right. Really, I am. It's just—' She broke off, unable to go on for the moment. 'We should have found her by now. It's so cold out here, too exposed to the elements. She's too small to be out here on her own, she's just a baby.'

'Don't give up on her, Jenna,' he said coaxingly. 'She can't have gone too far. We'll just keep going until we find her.'

'I know.' She sniffed. 'I'm sorry…I just keep thinking that she might be afraid and crying and wondering why no one is looking for her…'

Overcome, she buried her head in Ross's chest. He stroked her hair, pressing a tender kiss on her brow. His lips were gentle and comforting, and Jenna was glad that they hadn't split up to search for the child, that he was here with her now.

'Do you remember when you and Alex were children,' he murmured, 'and you went off to climb the rocks at the foot of the cliffs near MacInnes Bluff? You couldn't have been much more than five or six.'

She nodded slowly. 'We'd been out for the day with some family friends. Alex and I went off to look for crabs in the rock pools, and then we decided it would be fun to climb up on the rocks and play a game...pirates, I think. Alex was Captain Hook, if I remember right. He insisted I was his captive.'

'He would,' Ross said with a crooked smile. 'You slipped further and further away until you were out of sight, and by the time anyone realised you'd gone you were nowhere around. They were frantic with worry.'

'We were having such fun to begin with...we just got carried away. We were halfway round the island before we realised it was getting dark and we didn't know how to get back. Then the tide started coming in and we climbed as high up as we could and hid in the caves.'

'I was getting really worried. I thought I'd never find you again. I thought of all the times I'd been impatient with you—you were a bundle of trouble, always wanting me to do this or that, wheedling, never taking no for an answer, never giving me any peace. But I hated it then, not knowing where you were or what had happened to you. I vowed if I found you, if you were all right, I'd never let you down, never tell you to go away. I'd just be thankful to have you around, noisy and a nuisance, or whatever. I would keep cool and simply be happy that you were safe.'

Jenna's sniffs turned to a strangled chuckle. 'That vow didn't last long, did it? As soon as you climbed up into that cave and saw us there you let rip. What were we thinking of? Didn't we know everyone on the island had been out half the night looking for us? But I was so relieved to see you there, even if you did look as mad as hell.'

'I wasn't angry for long—and certainly not with you. How could I be? You were safe and that was all that mattered. Alex should have known better. He was that little bit older, and he was thoroughly sheepish and ashamed of himself for not knowing how to get back, while you were just scared out of your wits. You'd lost your mother just a year or so before, and I felt so sorry for you...protective and concerned. I just wanted to wrap you up and take you back home with me.'

'I remember how it felt before you came along to rescue us. It was so dark, and I could hear the waves crashing against the rocks.' She gave an awkward grimace. 'Poor little Kirsty—she must be terrified.' She felt shaky again, her mouth trembling with unhappiness, and Ross held her close, looking down into her troubled eyes.

'You're upset because you know what it feels like to be lost, but remember we found you and Alex, and we will find Kirsty, believe me. Maybe she went trailing after the wild goats—she was always fascinated by them. Sometimes they look for shelter in the trees down by the loch. We could try there next.'

Jenna blinked doubtfully. 'That seems such a long

way for a small child to have wandered,' she said huskily.

But perhaps there was something in what Ross was saying. She braced her shoulders. 'You could be right, though. Perhaps that's what she did. We should at least go and make sure.'

'That's my girl,' he murmured. His gaze slid to the softness of her mouth, still wavering with a trace of uncertainty, and after a moment's hesitation he bent his head towards her and dropped a swift, insistent kiss on her lips.

He drew back, pulling in a deep breath as though to clear his head, then he looked at her and must have seen her dazed expression because he smiled briefly and said, 'No more doubts…promise me? We'll carry on looking.' His hand engulfed her smaller one. 'Let's go.'

Jenna found herself being swept along beside him. She wanted to focus on what they were doing, where they were going, but her mind was stunned, thrown into a state of shock by the impulsive, swift demand of that kiss. She could feel it even now in the throbbing of her mouth, in the rippling after-effects that reverberated through her limbs.

She tried to shake off the strange feelings that had come over her. It was just a kiss, she told herself. A wake-up-call, designed to bring her jerkily out of her despondency and back to the present.

How could Ross know that the mere touch of his mouth on hers had sent flame sparking like wildfire through her entire being?

CHAPTER FOUR

THE waters of the loch rippled with the murmurings of the wind, the moonlight sending silver beams over its surface, and as she stared out over the glassy expanse Jenna shivered again and huddled deeper into her coat.

'There's just a chance that she might have gone to shelter in the trees over there,' Ross said, looking to where the hills rose sombrely in the distance. 'We could try calling to her again.'

They walked in the direction of the wooded slopes, and they both called out Kirsty's name, but there was no answering cry and Jenna was becoming more and more anxious as they went on.

As they drew closer, Ross shone his torch into the trees, and they walked towards the woods where the leafy canopy closed over their heads, leaving them in a world of bewildering, gloomy darkness. Jenna was glad that Ross was by her side.

'There's a clearing further on in the woods where we used to play as children,' she said quietly. 'Perhaps we should head towards that. Kirsty might know the way if she's been there with her brother.'

Ross nodded. 'I remember it, but it all looks so different in the dark. We ought to try to keep note of any landmarks so that we can find our way out again.'

He shone the beam of light over the bent and twisted branches of a huge tree, then upwards and around, throwing up ghastly black shadows, and Jenna caught glimpses of the rugged heights all around. She could just make out the line of a dirt path snaking through the woodland.

'That way,' she said, sensing that if the child had come this way she might have followed a well-worn route.

'OK. We'll follow the path.' Ross reached for her hand once more, and she responded to the warmth of his touch, feeling a little more secure in his firm grasp.

The woods were scary in the black of night, there was only the crackle of twigs underfoot and the scrabbling sound of small animals scurrying for cover in the undergrowth. If Kirsty was in here somewhere, she must be terribly afraid.

Jenna called the little girl's name again, stopping to listen intently, but there was no answer from the child, and Jenna bit her lip, her gaze deeply troubled as she looked around.

Ross gently squeezed her hand as though he wanted to reassure her. 'Come on,' he said persuasively. 'We'll keep on looking. It's best if we keep moving.'

She pulled in a steadying breath, and was about to go on once more when she thought she heard a faint rustling sound mingled with what might have been a soft murmur. It was so indistinct that she couldn't be sure, but it was somehow different to the usual night sounds, and she frowned, standing very still and listening carefully.

'What was that?' she whispered. 'Did you hear that?' She looked up at Ross and saw him frown.

'I heard something, but I'm not sure what it was.'

They listened again, then Ross called out, 'Kirsty...where are you? Sweetheart, shout if you're there and we'll come and find you.'

They were silent again, waiting for what seemed like an eternity, but there was no more sound, and Jenna's stomach lurched uneasily, becoming leaden inside her.

Her heart began to thump heavily, and she fine-tuned her senses to take in everything around her. 'I'm sure I heard something a few minutes ago,' she said urgently. 'Whatever it was, I think it came from over there. I'm going to take a look.'

'Slow down, it's rough going around here. We don't want you breaking a leg.'

They made their way over a rise in the ground, and then discovered that the land dropped away steeply down to a clearing where a gnarled tree dipped a thick branch until it almost touched the earth.

'Down there—take care that you don't lose your footing.' Ross led the way, moving down the slope with careful steps, bracing himself against the gradient and planting his feet firmly against the curling roots of the trees with every step. He held out his arm to Jenna, lending support as she made her way down and steadying her when she might have slipped.

'I'm OK,' she said breathlessly. 'Thanks.' She peered into the gloom, but it was hard to distinguish anything among the crooked shapes of the trees and the rugged terrain.

At the foot of the slope, Ross shone the torch around once more, and she realised all at once that they had found the clearing. In a sudden flicker of the light she caught sight of an oddly shaped mound.

'What was that?' She pointed. 'Over there.'

He flashed the beam of light around once more, and up against a shadowy hollow in a tree trunk Jenna saw a little bundle of what looked like rags.

Moving towards it, she knelt down to take a closer look and realised with a sense of shock that it was the child. Kirsty's small figure was huddled against the roots of the tree, her T-shirt and dungarees looking grey in the darkness.

'Oh, no... Oh, you poor baby.' With gentle fingers she touched the child's slender arm and leg, and choked back a sob of distress. 'Ross,' she said brokenly, 'she's half-frozen.' She bent her head to the little girl's chest, and found that she was barely breathing. Her face was puffy and her lips a bluish-grey.

'She must be hypothermic,' she whispered to Ross. 'Lying out here in the cold, her temperature must have dropped way below the norm. And there's a cut on her head where she must have banged it. I think she might have tripped and knocked her head on the tree.'

Jenna stroked the child's soft curls. 'Poor little darling,' she whispered. 'We've found you now. We'll look after you, I promise.' She spoke softly, tenderly, but Kirsty didn't seem to hear the quiet words and she wasn't reacting in any way, not even to make a murmur as Jenna carefully tested her pulse.

Ross studied the child's still body and said grimly, 'She might be concussed.' He checked the undergrowth close by, adding, 'It looks as though she's been sick at some point. We don't know what damage she did when she fell. I'd better put a collar round her neck to support the cervical spine, just in case. Let me see what you put in the holdall. There might be something in there that I can use.'

'There's a hand towel—I just threw it in because I thought it might come in handy. That should roll up well enough.'

He dug in the bag and pulled the fleecy towel out, then worked quickly but carefully to put the makeshift collar in place to support Kirsty's neck. 'Let's get the blanket around her and take her back to the cottage as fast as we can so that we can get her warmed up. It's nearest to here, and it's closer than the surgery.'

Jenna nodded, and pulled the blanket from her holdall with shaking fingers. She wrapped Kirsty in it, taking care to cover her head where the loss of warmth would be greatest. Ross took off his jacket and wrapped that around the child, too, before taking out his mobile phone.

'I'll let the police know that we've found her.'

Jenna glanced at him briefly, before turning back to the little girl. At least he was wearing a reasonably thick sweater. She didn't want to be worrying about him catching his death as well.

With infinite care she lifted Kirsty into her arms, tenderly cuddling her so that she could instil some warmth and comfort into the frail little body. The little girl was very still, totally unresponsive, and Jenna was suddenly desperately afraid that they might be too late. The pulse was barely discernible, and there was the terrible danger that her heart might stop beating altogether.

She cradled the little girl so that her own body heat would help, but when Ross had finished making the

call he said, 'Let me take her. I can handle her weight
better than you can over this rough ground. We need
to hurry…'

He didn't say, Before it's too late, but Jenna knew
only too well what the danger was. They had to get
the child's body temperature back to normal or the
consequences were too dire to contemplate. As it was,
Kirsty was almost lifeless in Ross's arms, and his
expression was as bleak as Jenna had ever seen it.

'I've asked the officer to call for an ambulance,' he
said as they hurried back the way they had come.

He held Kirsty firmly in the crook of his arm and
tried to help Jenna up the steep slope, but she waved
him away and managed on her own, wanting him to
give all his attention to the child.

'They'll meet us at the cottage. She'll be better off
in hospital, but at least we'll be able to do what we
can at the cottage to stabilise her condition before we
send her off there.'

Jenna was concerned about the move to the hospital, which was on the mainland, but Ross was
right—it had to be done if Kirsty was to get the care
she needed. There was always the risk that the child's
heart would go into an abnormal rhythm, and the hospital would be the best place to monitor her condition
if that should happen.

It wouldn't be a simple move. The ambulance de-
pot was at the far side of the island, and when the
ambulance arrived they would need to have arrangements in place to ferry the child across the sea to the
mainland. There would be another ambulance journey
from there to the hospital.

Ross held Kirsty securely as they made their way

back through the woods towards the road, holding her close to his body so that he could shield her from the wind. Jenna glanced at him, seeing the worry in his dark eyes, and quickened her steps.

The road to the cottage was fairly steep, and hard going, but they covered the distance in quick time, and Jenna was enormously relieved to see the cottage outlined on the rise of the hill.

'I'm glad I thought to light the fire in the sitting room,' she said as she hurriedly unlocked the front door and the warmth met them. 'Take her in there. Put her on the settee and try to make her comfortable. I'll go and get more blankets.'

'My emergency medical kit is in the boot of the car.' He tossed her a set of car keys, and she grabbed them and hurried out.

She was back in a couple of minutes, and by then Ross had settled the little girl amongst the soft cushions, not too close to the heat of the fire, because that would cause her temperature to rise too fast and that was something they had to avoid. It could cause peripheral vasodilatation which might lead to shock and possibly death.

Kirsty's breathing was still giving them cause for concern, and Ross worked swiftly to put an endotracheal tube in place so that they could give her oxygen.

'I'll set up an IV line,' Jenna said. If they gave Kirsty warmed fluids intravenously, it would help increase her body temperature.

'It won't be easy.' Ross winced. 'Her body's in shock and her circulation's shutting down...but I've loosened the blankets around her foot so that we can have a go.'

'I'll do it.' She understood his reservations, of course. Children's veins were so tiny, and the effects of shock on the child's system could make it difficult to slip in the cannula. Even though she'd spent many months working in paediatrics, before going into general practice, and it was a procedure she'd followed many times, she was always relieved when the tube was safely in place.

She worked efficiently now, with Ross helping to tape the tube securely and hook up the fluids. His gentle smile, and murmured, 'Well done,' when they had finished made her flush in pleased response in spite of her anxiety.

The police arrived a few minutes later, along with the ambulance, and then they were both kept busy, overseeing the transfer of the child to the waiting vehicle and dealing with the officer who'd been in charge of the search.

Kirsty's parents had followed the ambulance, and were understandably distressed to see their little girl in such a bad way. Ross did his best to soothe them, while Jenna spoke to the paramedics.

She watched them wrap the little girl in space blankets, which would retain maximum heat, and supervised the monitoring of heart activity and blood pressure.

'On top of everything else, there's always the possibility of a chest infection setting in,' she said quietly, 'but we've given her an antibiotic to try to ward off pneumonia.' Then, as the parents came into the ambulance to be with their daughter, she stood to one side.

Kirsty's mother held the child's hand and kissed

her cheek, while all the time tears ran in silvery streaks down her face. The father looked ashen, not saying a word but never taking his eyes off his little girl. Jenna could only imagine how dreadful they must be feeling.

Ross appeared at the doors of the ambulance, and when she climbed down to stand beside him on the road he said quietly, 'Will you hold the fort for me for a couple of hours, Jenna? I'd like to stay with her until she gets to the hospital.'

'Of course. Just divert any calls to me.' Her expression was suddenly troubled. 'You will let me know how she is?'

'I will.' He paused, then gently pressed her shoulder with his hand, his thumb stroking lightly over her collar-bone, and said, 'You were brilliant, the way you worked with her. I'm just thankful you were there with me today, and I'm sure it helped, both of us trying to think where she might be. It would have been hellish for either one of us to come across her like that alone, wouldn't it? It was good to know that you were by my side when we found her. As it was, we made a team... We worked well together, didn't we?'

Jenna nodded, too full of emotion to say any more just then, and Ross turned and climbed into the ambulance. She waited as the paramedic closed the doors behind him, and watched until the vehicle disappeared from view on the winding road. Then she went back into the cottage.

An odd restlessness had come over her, and although it was late she was finding it hard to settle after the night's events. Maybe a hot chocolate drink would help.

She quickly tidied up the sitting room, then went into the kitchen, waiting while the milk heated on the burner, and stared abstractedly out of the window into the darkness beyond.

Taking her cup over to the table, she came across Ross's jacket on a chair. Presumably the paramedics had left it there when they'd covered the little girl with the space blankets, and Ross had been too busy to notice it.

Would he come by to collect it? She lightly fingered the soft suede. Perhaps not. It would be very late by the time he arrived back on the island.

She sat in an armchair in the sitting room and tried to read for a while, but her thoughts were distracted by memories of the merciless cold of the woodland and the vulnerable four-year-old girl.

She found herself occasionally glancing up at the clock. Ross had probably thought better of calling her. He had more than likely gone straight home, meaning to give her an update at the surgery in the morning.

Jenna tried not to let her disappointment get the better of her. After all, it was already the early hours of the morning, and she couldn't sensibly expect him to take time out to come back to the cottage, or even to phone her.

Eventually, she went into the bathroom to brush her teeth and comb out the tangles in her hair, and it was then, as she was putting on her soft woollen dressing gown, that she heard a tapping on the front door. Her heartbeat quickened.

'Jenna...are you still up?' Ross's voice was subdued and low, as though he didn't want to disturb her, but she pulled the robe around herself and went quickly to the door, her spirits lifting a little because he'd come after all.

He looked pale and weary, standing there, with shadows of fatigue fanning out around his eyes, and she felt a desperate urge to hug him to her and soothe away all the anxieties left by the upheaval and trauma of the day.

He smiled tiredly when he saw her, and followed her through to the sitting room, where the hot embers of the fire still smouldered in the grate.

'I was beginning to think you wouldn't come,' she said softly.

His expression was wry. 'I nearly had second thoughts,' he murmured, sinking down onto the sofa where she'd ushered him, 'but I saw that your light was still on, and I wondered if you might be up after all.'

He searched her face, seeing her pale, anxious look, and said with a frown, 'You should have gone to bed.'

'I couldn't. I wanted to know how Kirsty is, whether she managed to stand up to the journey all right. Has there been any change?'

'Her temperature's up slightly, but they're worried about her heart rhythm, and they needed to check out the bang to her head as well. There's a slight fracture to the skull, so they're being ultra-cautious.'

He grimaced. 'I don't suppose the journey helped, but we simply don't have the facilities here on the island to do any more. I wanted to stay longer at the hospital, but it was getting very late and there's surgery in the morning. I have to try to get some sleep, if only a few hours. We should get to know something more tomorrow.'

'I suppose so.' She paced the floor restlessly. 'Her parents must be beside themselves with worry—the brother, too. How is he bearing up, do you know?'

He grimaced. 'Connor feels guilty as hell for losing track of her, from all accounts. Apparently, he went to the farm to work on a tractor that needed fixing. He'd thought it would be just a simple job that wouldn't take him above an hour, and Kirsty had badgered him as usual to take her along with him for the ride. She loves visiting farms, and seeing all the animals, especially at this time of year when the young ones are around.'

Ross moved his hands in a gesture of resignation. 'Of course, these things never work out as you want them to, do they? The job took much longer than Connor had expected, and Kirsty decided to go and play in the barn. He checked on her from time to time and then the farmer's daughter came home and took her in the house for milk and cake. A mix-up happened somehow, and they each thought the other was looking after her.' His mouth turned down at the corners. 'We know the rest.'

'It makes me want to weep, just thinking about it.' Jenna swallowed on the lump that swelled in her throat, and saw that he was equally disturbed by the way things had turned out. He shifted in his seat and stretched his taut muscles, and she thought he was about to get to his feet.

She said quietly, 'Stay there. You look worn out. Sit and rest yourself while I go and make you a hot drink.' Her gaze narrowed on him quizzically. 'I don't suppose you've eaten anything in the last few hours, have you?'

His brows made an odd quirk as he thought about that. 'Do you know—I forgot all about it?'

Jenna's mouth twitched. 'That won't have helped. It's no wonder you're dead on your feet. I'll go and make some sandwiches. You stay put.'

He sank back on the settee. 'That sounds tempting. Thanks. You're an angel.'

She sent him a sweet smile. 'I'll remind you that you said that…'

She went into the kitchen, the smile still playing around her mouth. He was a good man, caring and thoughtful, and she was so glad that he'd taken the trouble to come back to the cottage to tell her what was happening when he might simply have gone straight home. The very least she could do was feed him.

But when she went back into the sitting room a few minutes later, she saw that his eyes were closed and his face was relaxed in sleep. He looked wonderfully peaceful and content, and she stood there and watched him for a while before the sound of a log falling gently on the fire brought her thoughts back to practicalities.

Ross had slumped a little to one side on the sofa, and she put the tea tray she was holding down onto the low table and went to place a cushion by his shoulder so that he could rest more comfortably.

She moved quietly, taking care not to disturb him, but he opened his eyes as she tucked the cushion in place, blinking as he took in his surroundings and then gradually registered where he was.

He smiled drowsily at her. 'I'm sorry, I didn't mean to fall asleep on you.' He yawned and stretched, easing his stiffening muscles. 'How long was I out of it?'

'Only a few minutes. Don't worry about it.' She pushed the plate of sandwiches across the table towards him, and said, 'Try to eat something. It will make you feel better.'

He reached for the plate, offering it to her. 'Share them with me.'

'All right.' She sat beside him on the sofa and poured tea, and they ate in companionable silence for a while. Another log crackled on the fire and sent a shower of sparks shooting upwards.

He watched it for a moment or two, absorbing the warmth, then said soberly, 'I wouldn't like to go through many days like today. It's bad enough when adults are seriously ill—you try to stay professional and do your job, without letting your emotions get in the way—but when it's a child, how can anyone be unaffected? It really tears me apart when a young child is desperately sick.'

He ran his thumb absently around the rim of his cup, then said, 'I don't think I could ever have stayed for any length of time in paediatrics as you did. I just know it would have been too much for me to handle.'

His expression was sombre for a moment, but when he looked at her again a faint smile twisted his mouth. 'And yet you do it so well. You seem to take everything in your stride. I watched you today, and I could see how good you are at what you do. Even though you're affected by what you have to deal with, it doesn't affect your ability to cope.'

'I wouldn't say it was that simple,' Jenna answered huskily. 'We all cope when we have to. You certainly did. For myself, there were times when I wondered what on earth I was doing, specialising in caring for sick children.'

'Were there? Tell me about it.'

She said slowly, 'No one can work with youngsters who are very ill without going through some desperately wretched times. I got by for a long time because I realised that I could at least try to make a real difference to their lives while I was there. I would do my job as well as possible, do my utmost to pull them through, and hopefully help them back to full health.'

She sent him a quick smile. 'It's a wonderful feeling when you see a child who was dreadfully ill start to fight his way back, isn't it? I'm always amazed by how resilient they are. They're so plucky...and you feel such a rush of joy when you see them up and about again.'

'I can understand that.' Ross sent her a searching glance. 'You knew from the beginning what you wanted to do, and you worked hard to be successful. But, after all that, you chose to go into general practice. Why did you do that if you felt so strongly about it?'

She was thoughtful for a time, not certain that she could explain it properly. 'I suppose it was because, like you, I couldn't have gone on dealing with such a constant level of trauma. It can be heart-rending. But I knew that they were planning to build the new paediatric centre where I'm working in Perth, and I'm hoping that I can have the best of both worlds if I get the job I've applied for there.'

Jenna's green gaze took on a soft glow as she thought about it. 'I would be working with mothers and their babies, and I'd be taking the children's clinics on a very regular basis. In a way, the fact that I've specialised in the past should help me to do the job better by giving me more of an insight into what can go wrong—and where best to pick up any potential problems than in a child health clinic? I've wanted to do this job for a long time now.'

'I know you have.' Something flickered in the depths of his eyes, a kind of tension, an unease. She couldn't be sure what it was, but it was gone in a moment and he said with quiet conviction, 'You'll get the job, I'm sure of it. They'd be fools not to take you on.' He quickly drained the rest of his tea and put his empty cup back on the table with a snap.

'You would say that,' she said with a smile. 'You're prejudiced. You haven't seen the competition.'

Ross didn't return the smile, but stared into the dying embers of the fire for a moment or two, then said seriously, 'You're good at your job. You've the right kind of experience, and you've worked with the people at the medical centre and they think well of you there. I don't see that there can be any doubt. You'll get this job, it'll be good for you, and you'll be the best thing that ever happened for the people there.'

Briskly, he pushed his plate away and got to his feet. 'Thanks for the supper, it was delicious. I should be going now, though. I have to be up early to deal with a number of things before surgery, and you need

to get some rest. I've kept you up far too late as it
is.'

'That doesn't matter.' She quelled the sudden sense
of disappointment that rose in her as he made to
leave. Of course he couldn't stay. It was madness to
think that he might even have wanted to, but for a
brief moment part of her had wanted him to stay with
her like this, together in the warm comfort of her cosy
sitting room for much, much longer.

His jacket was still on the back of the chair in the
kitchen, and she gathered it up and handed it to him.
'Don't forget this.'

'Thanks,' he murmured. 'You should get to bed
now. You've had a long day.'

'I will.'

She moved to stand beside him, and murmured
huskily, 'I'm glad you came back to tell me what was
happening. Thanks for that, Ross.'

On an impulse she reached up to kiss him lightly
on the cheek, and he was still for just a moment before his arms closed around her. Then he hugged her
to him, flame flickering in the depths of his smoke-
blue eyes as he stared down at her. Then his mouth
came down on hers in a brief, fierce kiss that seared
her lips with its stunning intensity and took her breath
away.

She registered the warmth of his caress through all
the nerve endings in her body with a vibrant, heady
rush of exhilaration that made her want to cling to
him, to have their bodies merge as one. But then, just
as swiftly as the contact had begun, he broke off the
kiss and released her. Her lips ached for him still, but
he was turning away already, leaving her with only

the fragments of his taut smile as he started to walk briskly to the door.

She wanted to say something, anything, to have him come back to her, to have him stay with her, but the words wouldn't come. Instead, she saw him out to his car and watched him drive away before she slowly turned back towards the house. She was bewildered by his leave-taking, by the sudden surge of passion that had flared between them, only to be dissolved just as quickly in the cold blast of night air. What was going through his mind? Was he regretting that kiss already? Perhaps he'd only kissed her that way because all the emotions that were locked up inside him were demanding release after the desperate evening they'd spent together looking for the child.

Wearily, Jenna went back into the house. She felt exhausted now, more tired than she'd ever been, but somehow she didn't think that sleep would come easily that night.

Perhaps working with Ross hadn't been such a good idea after all. It had brought back to her all the old memories of how much she'd enjoyed being with him when she'd lived on the island with her father, of all the good times they'd shared. But that would all soon come to an end, wouldn't it, when she went back to the mainland?

He was even encouraging her to go for the new job, certain that it was right for her. And it was, wasn't it? She'd gone after it with her eyes wide open, full of enthusiasm and determination, and nothing had happened to make her change her mind about that, had it?

So why was she now feeling suddenly so very much at odds with herself?

CHAPTER FIVE

JENNA phoned the hospital from the surgery on Friday morning to find out if there had been any change in Kirsty's condition, but there wasn't a lot to tell. The little girl was in the intensive care unit, and they were monitoring her condition constantly.

'I keep wondering if she might have stood a better chance if we'd been able to treat her on the island,' Jenna said bleakly as she relayed the news to Ross.

'I've had the same worries,' he agreed with a frown. 'I'm constantly arguing the case for a cottage hospital out here, given the increasing number of tourists that we have each year, along with the rising birth rate, but nothing much comes of it. There never seems to be enough funding available.'

Grim-faced, he added, 'So far we've managed to avoid any fatalities in patients being transferred—but how much longer we can go on doing that, I wouldn't like to say. In the meantime, all I can do is keep banging on the door of the powers that be.'

Jenna wished there was something she could do, but since she was as helpless in this as he was she said, 'At least Kirsty's condition seems to be relatively stable for the moment, and that's something to be thankful for, I suppose. Apparently the fracture caused some swelling around the brain, so they're giving her drugs to counteract that.' She winced.

'Poor child, she's been through an awful time. Her parents must be feeling terrible.'

Mairi poured coffee for all of them, and said, 'The grandfather's coming in for an appointment later this morning. I know he's not been well lately, but I suspect it's more that he wants to talk about the wee child than anything else.'

Ross nodded. 'It's understandable. I wondered if he might come in. The parents are still at the hospital, so he's been left alone to dwell on things—he's bound to want some contact with us. He thinks the world of Kirsty.'

He frowned, glancing down at his watch. 'I've some urgent home visits to make this morning. I'm not sure whether I'll be back by the time he comes in.'

His gaze meshed with Jenna's. 'Do you think you could talk to him for me for now, and I'll have a word with him this afternoon? I really ought to see these patients myself—one of them is quite elderly and might be confused if someone else goes along to see him, and the other, Jeannie MacDonald, has a nasty kidney infection from the sound of things.'

He glanced at the message pad. 'My mother rang to tell me she was worried about her—they've been the best of friends for ages, and she sounded quite anxious about things. I want to take a look just to reassure myself it's not going to develop into anything worse.'

'That's all right,' Jenna said quickly. 'I'll speak to him. I'll do what I can to put him in the picture about what's happening, and try to comfort him as best I can.'

'Thanks.' He gave her a quick smile. 'I knew I could rely on you to hold the fort.'

'Of course you can.' She hesitated, then said, 'If you talk to Flora, will you ask her if she'd like to come over to the cottage next time she comes into town? I've tried phoning, but she must have been out of the house whenever I've called. Any afternoon—I should be in for most of the week. I want to get on with painting the bedrooms.'

'I'll ask Annie to mention it to her when she goes over there this morning.'

'Oh...well, yes, that's fine.'

It was only natural that Annie was a big part of his life, but it didn't *feel* fine at all. She winced inwardly. Ross's private life had nothing to do with her, did it? She ought not to delve into things, she knew that, but curiosity got the better of her, and she couldn't help asking, 'Will you be seeing Annie, then?'

'I said I'd call in to take a look at her younger brother—he wasn't one hundred per cent well when I was there the other night, and now it looks as though he might have taken a turn for the worse. She sounded quite concerned about him.'

Of course he would see Annie on a regular basis. What had she expected? Jenna was beginning to wish she hadn't started any of this, but now she asked, 'Who's going to be looking after him while Annie's at your mother's place?'

'Oh, Annie's parents will be back by now, I should think. They'd made arrangements to stay at a hotel for a couple of nights—they were celebrating their friends' wedding anniversary and Annie volunteered to babysit. He's eleven years old, mind, so that didn't go down with him too well.' His mouth curved in a wry smile, and Jenna tried to respond in kind, putting a clamp on her wavering emotions.

'He gave you some problems, did he?'

'Not for too long. I know he's into computers, so I took a game along with me. That caused a bit of a clash, because Annie had cooked up a wonderful supper and all he could think about was bolting the food down so he could play it.' He grinned. 'It kept him happy for most of the evening, though, and Annie and I had the chance to talk.'

'It all worked out, then.' Had the evening extended into the night? Jenna's spirits plunged to new depths, just thinking about the possibility.

Ross left to make his rounds just a few minutes later, and she had to make a determined effort to get herself into a businesslike frame of mind ready for the morning ahead. She went into her room and rang for the first patient.

It wasn't a difficult surgery, for which she was thankful after the bad night, and she'd dealt with a fair number on her list before James Blake, Kirsty's grandfather, put his head round the door.

'You were at Flora's house the other day,' he said, coming in and sitting opposite her. He tried a smile, but his face looked grey and careworn this morning, and she could understand how wretched he must be feeling.

'That's right...and you had Kirsty with you. I'm so sorry about what happened yesterday, James.' She covered his hand lightly with her own, and saw a glimmer of tears blur his eyes.

'She's such a sweet, bonny little girl. Always full

of fun, wanting to show you this and that. Never stops asking questions.'

His voice was breaking and his jaw worked awkwardly. 'And now the poor mite's in hospital, not knowing anything of what's going on around her. I cannae believe this is happening... I cannae sleep, or eat. I'm having trouble even trying to think straight.'

'Is there anything I can do to help?' Jenna asked with gentle concern, understanding how very difficult things must be for him just now. 'If it's all too much for you, I could prescribe a sedative.'

'No, lass. I'll get by. I just felt I had to come in and thank you for all that you and Dr Buchanan did for the child last night. If you hadn't found her when you did...'

He broke off, unable to go on, and Jenna put an arm around him and waited for him to recover himself.

'How are you feeling otherwise?' she asked in a while. 'In yourself, I mean.'

She glanced at the notes on her computer screen and saw that Ross had prescribed anti-inflammatories for an arthritic condition that was affecting his neck and causing him pain. 'Are the tablets helping?'

'Och, I stopped taking them because I was feeling a bit dizzy sometimes, and my hands were tingling. Side effects, I suppose. But I'm not complaining, you know. I didn't come here to talk about myself, I just wanted to thank you both. I'll maybe talk to Dr Buchanan when he comes in later.'

'Yes, he said he'd like to have a word. Let me take your blood pressure while you're here,' she murmured, wrapping the cuff around his arm when he made no objection.

He was glad of the chance to talk for a while, she guessed, and she wanted to give him the opportunity to offload some of his anxieties.

'Your blood pressure's OK,' she said when she'd finished. 'I'll just have a listen to your chest. Have you been getting any pain there, or discomfort of any kind?'

He hadn't, it seemed, and after she'd examined him she was reasonably satisfied that his dizziness wasn't being caused by any underlying heart problem.

'It isn't likely that the tablets will be causing the dizziness and the tingling,' Jenna told him, 'but we'll do a blood test just to be on the safe side, as it's a few months since you last had one. It's more likely that the inflammation and swelling in your neck are causing those symptoms, and the tablets should help to make you feel better after a while. I could prescribe a different kind of anti-inflammatory, though, if you like.'

'Och, no, don't bother, lass. I'll stick with the ones I've got for a bit longer, if you think they're all right.'

He stood up, and reached for her hand. 'I won't take up any more of your time. I just needed to come in and say thank you for finding my wee girl. If there's ever anything I can do for you, just let me know.'

Jenna clasped his hand in return. 'I hope you hear good news soon.'

Normally, she was happy enough to stay at the surgery and talk to Mairi during the lunch-break, but today she was in a hurry to go back to the cottage.

She needed some time on her own so that she could think, and she planned to get on with the decorating. Painting had always been a therapeutic occupation for her, and brightening up the bedroom would help her to work through the strain of the last few hours.

Ross drove up to the house after she'd been home for not much more than an hour, when she was adding the finishing touches to the bedroom window frame.

She saw him climb out of the car and look up, and when he discovered that she was perched on an upstairs sill, leaning out to add a final coat of white gloss to the frame, his mouth made a firm line.

'I might have known I'd come along and find you hanging out of a window or doing something equally reckless,' he called up to her, his brows meeting in a dark scowl.

She waved back at him, the paintbrush making wobbly swirls in the air. 'I'll be down in a jiffy. Just give me a minute.'

She eased herself off the sill and tried to smooth down her jeans and T-shirt. Was she looking too much of a mess? She hoped she hadn't transferred any of the paint to herself.

As it was, her hair was in a haphazard state, loosely pinned up in an effort to keep it out of harm's way, but stray tendrils had escaped to curl about her face and temples, and she tried unsuccessfully to blow them away. Quickly she rinsed her hands and went to open the door.

Ross's mocking glance travelled over her in swift assessment, missing nothing. 'At least you're all in one piece. Why on earth were you up there, doing a balancing act?'

'No ladder,' she explained with an expansive gesture of her hands. 'There was a hitch in deliveries at the hardware store. I'll have to get one so that I can do the rest of the frames, but I didn't want to miss out on the dry weather.'

Flora was with him, and Jenna gave her a pleased smile and a hug, then looked at her carefully, noting the drawn lines on her face.

'I'm so glad you could come over here, Flora,' she said, bringing her into the house. 'How are you? You look a bit tired—you haven't been overdoing things, have you?'

'Oh, no, my dear.' Flora patted her hand. 'I haven't been sleeping too well just lately, that's all. I've been a bit worried about my friend Jeannie. She's been very poorly with a fever, and she's in a lot of pain.'

Jenna nodded, frowning, and looked at Ross. 'Is that the lady you were going to see this morning?'

'That's right. She's not very well at all, but I've given her some tablets that should help. Mum wants to go and stay with her for a day or two so that she can look after her.'

She turned back to Flora. 'That sounds like a good idea, if you're sure you can manage.'

'I'll do fine. At least I'll be able to keep an eye on her. She's been such a good friend to me over the years. Ross is going to drive me over there later—I used to be able to drive myself, you know, but after the accident with my hip I get a bit too stiff to sit behind a wheel for long.'

'In the meantime,' Ross put in, 'you two will have the chance to get your heads together for an hour or so. My first appointment for afternoon surgery isn't until four o'clock, so that gives us a while.'

Jenna smiled. 'I'll put the kettle on and make some tea,' she said, busying herself. 'It won't take long, the water's hot already. Flora, take the weight off your feet, and have a look at that home and country magazine—there are some wonderful landscapes in there.' She pushed the magazine across the table towards her.

Ross took off his jacket and draped it over a chair. 'While you're both occupied, I'll go and finish off the painting you were doing. That way I shan't have to worry about you breaking your neck while I'm away.'

She flapped a hand at him. 'You don't need to do that. I've finished doing the frames now, and the walls can wait until tomorrow.'

'I'm good at walls,' he said with a grin. 'Think of it as a kind of thank you for all the work you've done at the surgery.'

Her mouth twitched. 'I'm being paid for that. Honestly, you don't have to help. Besides...' she gave him a quick once-over '...you're not dressed for it.'

He was wearing casual clothes, but the trousers were beautifully cut and the shirt was made from a fine linen. Not at all the sort of materials you'd want to mix with paint and turpentine.

'I've an old sweater in the car. Don't worry about it.'

'But I can manage on my own—'

'I know you can. But I want to do it, so I'd appreciate it if you'd stop arguing and let me get on.' He flicked a glance at the kettle steaming gently on the burner. 'Water's boiling.'

He started to head upstairs and tossed back, 'What colour do you want on these walls?'

He wasn't going to take no for an answer, was he? Jenna threw him an exasperated glance, turned off the heat under the kettle and followed him up the stairs.

'Sunset glow,' she told him, walking into her bedroom and waving a hand towards the big divan bed, 'to blend with the ginger and apricot bedspread.'

He rolled his eyes in response. 'It figures,' he drawled. 'Strong, warm colours. That's one way to liven up a Scottish winter's night.'

'I suppose you have a better suggestion?'

Ross leaned negligently against the wardrobe, watching her in a leisurely fashion, his blue eyes dancing with wicked flame. 'Do you really want me to answer that?'

Jenna's cheeks flushed a hectic pink at the soft challenge in his voice. Suddenly, she didn't think it would be altogether wise to follow this line of thinking... She wasn't sure she could cope with Ross being provocative...unless he meant it...unless he was serious about her...and wanted her...really, really wanted her... Her mind went hazy at the mere thought.

'I expect you're full of ideas,' she managed in a thready voice. 'You'd know a lot more about that kind of thing than I do...' She turned away, but not quickly enough to miss the low rumble of his laughter, and the next moment he'd covered the distance between them, his arm sliding around her waist, drawing her back towards him.

'"That kind of thing?"' He was still chuckling softly, his warm breath lightly fanning the slender col-

umn of her neck, his hand spanning out over her ribcage, his thumb gently grazing the fullness of her
breast and playing havoc with all her attempts to think
clearly. 'You sound like a complete innocent, a sweet
young virgin who's experienced nothing more than a
few tender kisses and whispered sweet nothings... Is
that how it is with you, Jenna?' His lips gently
brushed the velvet curve of her neck, throwing her
senses into wild disarray. 'You are so lovely,' he murmured huskily. 'So irresistible. And you taste delicious, like the sweetest, purest honey...'

He turned her in his arms, looking down at her
softly parted lips, and his blue gaze became suddenly
intense as he said in a thick mutter, 'Somehow I don't
think a few light kisses would be nearly enough...'

Her heart slammed against her ribcage as she read
the message in his smoke dark eyes, but just as she
might have melted into his firm embrace he made a
juddery sigh and held her away from him so that she
felt the loss of his warm, solid presence like an acute
pain.

'You're teasing me,' she whispered huskily.
'You're making fun of me—that isn't fair.'

'Would I do that, Jenna?'

The soft gleam in his eyes confused her, and she
forced herself to take a steadying breath. 'I don't understand you. I don't know what you're thinking.'

He gave a low, self-mocking laugh. 'Nor did I for
a moment back there. But what I do know is that this
is neither the time nor the place, especially with my
mother downstairs.'

Jenna's mouth dropped open. 'Oh, Lord. I completely forgot.' She turned in an instant and fled from

the room, and the sound of his husky laughter followed her all the way down the stairs.

She went back to Flora feeling thoroughly agitated, but made a conscious effort to get herself back under control. Ross was in a purely mischievous mood, and she wouldn't let his teasing get to her.

Flora wanted to know all about her efforts to brighten up the cottage, and they spent the next hour or so going through swatches of material and pattern books and deciding what might look best. Jenna served up tea and cakes, and she was pleased to see that Flora looked a little better for her visit, though she was still concerned that she might be more frail than she made out.

With that on her mind, when Ross and Flora were preparing to leave some time later, she grabbed the opportunity to catch Ross alone and ask him if he thought there was any problem.

'I wondered if you'd notice anything,' he said in an undertone. 'She hasn't been her usual self just lately, but she won't hear of going back to the hospital for tests. I think she had enough of that when she broke her hip. I persuaded her to let me do a blood test and check her out in a very general way, but as for anything more I keep finding that I'm up against a brick wall.'

He winced. 'Maybe you might have more luck. Will you see her if I can get her to come into the surgery one day soon? She might confide in you more than she does in me.'

Jenna nodded. 'I'll do what I can. Perhaps we can persuade her to have a physical. Maybe Alex will bring her over one morning.'

'I'll ask him.' He rummaged in his pocket and drew out a key. 'While I think about it, you may as well have this.'

'What is it?'

'It's the key to the boathouse. You remember how to manage a motorboat, don't you?'

When she murmured agreement, he handed it over, saying, 'I bought a second boat some time ago so that Alex could come and go as he wanted, but there's no reason why you shouldn't use it whenever you want to. My mother has friends she can rely on to ferry her about if I'm not on hand. It can be awkward getting about the islands otherwise, and this way you'll be able to go over to the house whenever you want. You and Alex can sort it out between you.'

'Thanks.' She was touched by his consideration, and said quietly, 'That was very thoughtful of you.' On an afterthought, she asked, 'Has Alex settled in all right at home? I haven't seen much of him lately, but I expect he's studying for his exams.'

'Possibly.' His gaze narrowed on her thoughtfully. 'Does that trouble you—not seeing him? I know you've always been sweet on him.' She didn't answer him straight away, and he went on, 'From what I've heard, he's been helping out with things at the farm, as well as catching up with old friends, and he hasn't had much time to get his breath so far. I can't imagine that he'll stay away from you for very long, though.'

She blinked. 'I wasn't thinking about that.'

'Weren't you?' His look was disbelieving. 'You two were always inseparable.'

'Yes, we were. But we're both older now,' she said a little wistfully, thinking back to the times when they'd all been youngsters and had spent their days exploring the island with hardly a care in the world. 'Things change.'

He gave her a long look. 'They don't change that much. He's been telling me how you meet up for lunch in Perth sometimes, and get together for evenings out.'

'We do when we get the chance, but our schedules don't coincide all that often.'

'No?' He lifted a brow, then said laconically, 'Well, I wouldn't worry too much about that. They say absence makes the heart grow fonder, and maybe things will be different when the new wing opens at the health centre. You probably won't have to work late quite so often then.'

'Perhaps not...if I get the job.' She smiled. 'I think you're jumping the gun a bit.'

'Am I? We'll see.' He moved briskly towards the door. 'Thanks for talking to James this morning, by the way. I spoke to him earlier on the phone and said I'd go and spend the evening with him.'

'That should help. Do you want me to stay on call tonight?'

He shook his head. 'There's no need. If anything comes up I can deal with it.'

'OK.'

Since it looked as though she wasn't going to be called out this evening, Jenna decided to soak in a relaxing bath and then catch up on some reading. She still wasn't quite over the rigours of last night, but she was feeling much too restless to give in and go to bed.

Instead, she phoned the hospital for the latest report

on Kirsty and was told that the little girl was still very
poorly but showing some signs of recovery. Her temperature was much improved, and the swelling around
her brain wasn't quite so bad.

A bit more content now, she curled up in the armchair by the fire and tried to lose herself in the latest
best-seller which she'd picked up from the bookshop
in town.

When the phone rang an hour or so later she
frowned, wondering who it might be, and she was
startled to hear Alex's voice on the other end of the
line.

'Jen, can you come over here? To my mother's
house?' He sounded as though he was in a hurry.

'Why? Is something wrong?'

He laughed. 'No, nothing's wrong. I'm having
some friends round, that's all, and I thought you
might like to come and join us.'

She hesitated. 'I don't know about that, Alex. It's
dark already, and it would mean a boat ride. I'm not
sure I want to face that just now.'

'I'll come and fetch you,' he said swiftly, and she
was immediately suspicious.

'Something *is* wrong,' she said flatly. 'What is it?'

'Nothing, I promise you. I would have asked you
earlier, only we didn't decide to do anything until
about an hour ago.'

'When you realised Flora wasn't going to be coming home tonight, you mean?'

'I phoned and asked her and, anyway, she doesn't
mind me having friends round. Honestly, Jenna, I'd
love to have you come over for supper—you'll know
lots of the people here, and it will be great to meet

up with everyone. Aisleen said she might come over if she can get the grandparents to babysit.'

He paused, and she could almost hear his brain working. 'And while you're here, you could maybe help me out with the food,' he went on. 'I'm OK with the cold stuff, but there are sausage rolls and vol-au-vents in the deep freeze, and I haven't a clue what I'm supposed to do with them.'

That sounded more like the Alex she knew. 'You could try reading the packets,' she told him with a chuckle, but she knew she was wasting her breath, pointing that out. Alex had probably burned more ready meals than he could count.

'You'll come, though. I know you will,' he said triumphantly. 'I'll be there to pick you up in half an hour.'

He had clicked off before she had time to argue. Jenna smiled ruefully. Perhaps it wasn't such a bad idea after all. It would be good to meet up with Alex again and see her friends, and all she needed was a little time to put on some make-up and get dressed.

She was ready by the time Alex arrived. She'd put on a dove-grey top, shot through with lustrous threads, and a slim-fitting, slightly darker skirt.

'You look good,' he said appreciatively, giving her a hug and taking her out to the waiting car. 'I was hoping we'd have the chance to get together before this, but I've been too busy, one way and another.'

They set off on the drive to the jetty, and Jenna said, 'I know. Back in Perth, you said you have a lot of work to do, with your exams coming up soon. These will be your finals, won't they?'

He mumbled something and pulled a face, and she

sent him a sidelong glance, wondering what the problem was. 'What's the matter? Are you struggling?
Perhaps Ross can help.'

'I'd rather Ross didn't get involved. He's my
brother, and I love him, but, you know, he's always
been the one who succeeded, who got everything
right, and if I start thinking about the way he does
things, I'll just end up feeling even more of a failure.'

She stared at him. 'Why on earth should you think
of yourself as a failure? You've always done well,
once you set your mind to it.'

'That's it in a nutshell, really.' He grimaced as he
turned the car towards the harbour. 'I just can't seem
to get my mind around anything just lately. I think
about getting down to some work, and then I tell myself, what the hell, I'd sooner be seeing people and
having a good time.'

He laughed shortly, and cut the car's engine. 'And
it is good, having people around, having a few drinks,
getting merry.'

She smiled with him, but she sensed the underlying
insecurity that lay behind his expression. She knew
Alex very well, they'd been like brother and sister for
so many years, and she could see the faint glimmer
of uncertainty that flickered in his eyes before he
masked it with a show of bravado.

It wasn't quite the time to delve into what might
be troubling him, though, because they were kept
busy for the next few minutes, manoeuvring the boat
across the water, and as they approached his home
base Alex's mood seemed to lift.

In the farmhouse kitchen, she said brightly, 'So,

what food am I putting out, and when is everyone due to arrive?'

'I told people to come around nine—that will give us time to get organised. The drink's no bother, I've got most of everything that we want, but as to the food, I thought we'd just raid the freezer. I'll stock it up again afterwards.'

Luckily, there was enough to make a bit of a spread. Jenna worked swiftly to make sandwiches, heat up tasty treats and empty crisps and snacks into bowls, so that by the time people started to arrive at the house most of the preparations had been made.

She relaxed over the next couple of hours, though she couldn't help wishing that Ross was there with her. She hadn't expected to miss him quite so much, and her thoughts strayed to him often. But when she wondered how he might spend most of his evenings she was brought up cold, remembering Annie.

It had been some time since she'd been able to chat with old friends, though, and she made up her mind to make the most of it. Alex put himself in charge of the drinks and the CDs and there was a lot of dancing and laughter, and the hours flew by.

She was talking to Aisleen when one of the party-goers caught her attention, lurching forward and angrily aiming a swipe at a pint glass which stood on a table near her arm.

It happened so fast that there was nothing Jenna could do to stop it from falling, and Alex quickly pulled her to one side out of the way as the glass smashed to the floor.

They stared down at the shattered fragments. 'Has he had too much to drink, do you think?' Aisleen said worriedly, moving closer to Jenna as the man pushed past her.

Alex frowned as he watched him move away, then bent to clear up the mess.

Aisleen said, 'I just heard him accuse someone of taking his jacket. I don't remember seeing him with a jacket at all.'

Jenna glanced over at the man. Over the last half-hour he'd become steadily more abusive, though the abuse was aimed at no one in particular as far as she could tell.

'Neither do I. He was wearing a sweater when he arrived.'

He was in his mid-twenties, she guessed, and she thought he looked undernourished, his cheekbones prominent, the flesh of his face hollowed out. At the moment he looked agitated, though she couldn't have said who or what was the focus of his disturbed behaviour.

Alex got to his feet, putting the broken glass carefully into a bin. 'I think he's had rather a lot to drink. I noticed he had a bottle of whisky with him.'

'I don't think I recognise him,' Jenna said. 'Is he from around here?'

Alex shook his head. 'He came over with Tom on the ferry this morning. His name's Steve.'

His mouth tightened a fraction as he saw Steve eyeing up Flora's crystal vase as though it had done him a personal injury. 'I'll go and tell Tom to take him home.'

Jenna sipped a glass of fruit punch and chatted with Aisleen, casually observing the man from time to time over the next few minutes. She was worried he might get more violent.

Alex was doing his best to keep him from upsetting anyone, moving him into the study where he could talk to him quietly. After a few minutes, though, he came back to Jenna and said in a low voice, 'I think Steve must have cut himself on the broken glass. I'm not sure how bad it is...whether it might need stitching.'

'I can go and have a look at him, if you like.'

'Thanks, Jen. I'm sorry about this. Tom says he's never seen him like this before.'

She went with him to the study, asking softly, 'Do you know whether he might be taking drugs of some sort?'

He frowned. 'That had occurred to me, too. I don't think so, though. Aisleen just found the empty whisky bottle on the stairs.'

Jenna shrugged. 'Has she? It's probably just alcohol then—but it's important to check it's not drugs.'

'I'll ask Tom. He knows him better than anyone. He's with him now, in the study.'

Tom was struggling to keep Steve from breaking out of the room again, and from the fierce expression on Steve's face Jenna thought he might lash out at her. There was blood dripping from his wrist, she noticed, where the broken glass must have sliced him, and she went off to find her medical bag so that she could deal with the wound.

'It's deep enough, but not too serious,' she murmured as she put a dressing in place. 'You're lucky, Steve. You missed the main veins, or you might have done some real damage.'

She wasn't sure he knew what she was saying. He growled something in response, but she wasn't convinced that he was altogether conscious of where he was or what was going on around him. Still uncertain as to whether his condition might be drug related as well, she tried asking him a few questions, aimed at determining his mental status. In the end, she decided that he was probably too drunk to be coherent.

Directing her attention to Tom, she asked, 'Has he been taking any drugs, do you know?'

Tom hesitated, clearly unwilling to commit himself, and Jenna said quietly, 'I'm not here to pass judgement, Tom. I'm a doctor, and all that concerns me is that I give my patient the treatment he needs. I need to know exactly what he's taken so that I can be sure I'm doing the right thing.'

After a moment he said, 'It was diazepam. I told him he was a fool to drink with them, but he said he'd be all right.'

'Does he have any left? I'd like to see.'

'I'll go and look in his holdall.'

With Alex's help to keep him steady, she examined Steve, taking his blood pressure and listening to his heart, and after a minute or two Tom came back into the room and held out a package which contained tablets.

'OK,' Jenna said, taking a close look and satisfying herself that she knew what she was dealing with. 'Will you make sure you keep these safely for him?'

'I will.'

'Good. Do you know what medical condition he's being treated for?'

Tom nodded. 'I think the tablets were prescribed for anxiety.'

'All right. There's not much we can do for him right now except wait and see.'

She monitored Steve over the next quarter of an hour, until he'd calmed down.

'Will he be all right?' Alex asked, and she nodded, closing up her medical bag.

'I think so, as long as he stops drinking while he's on those tablets.' She turned to Tom. 'Take him home and let him sleep for a few hours. He should go and see his own doctor to tell him what happened and to have his dressing checked in the morning.'

Tom led Steve away, supporting him out to his car, and Alex helped Jenna to tidy up the things she'd used.

'I'm really glad you were here to sort him out,' Alex said, sounding relieved. 'He was getting out of hand, and I thought he might hurt someone, or himself.'

'Are you OK?' she asked, giving him an assessing look from under her lashes. 'I have the feeling you're not your usual self. What's wrong? Is it girl trouble?' Alex had dated a number of girls over the last few years, but none of his relationships seemed to work out in the long term.

He met her gaze briefly and gave an odd laugh, but then he said, 'I never could keep anything from you for long, could I?' His mouth twisted, and he said slowly, 'I have been seeing someone. She's great fun.'

He stopped talking, and Jenna lifted a brow. 'Go on, then. Tell me about her.'

He winced. 'Her name's Rebecca, and she works at one of the veterinary practices where I did some of my training. She's a nurse there.' He picked up the medical bag and placed it on the table. 'We got on well—she seemed to like me. We had some good times together—everything was a laugh, we have the same quirky sense of humour—but it all fizzled out.'

'Why, what happened?'

He shrugged awkwardly. 'I'm not sure. She started making excuses not to see me. Well...they sounded like excuses to me.'

That didn't sound like the normal pattern of things where Alex was concerned. He was usually the one to break hearts. 'Have you asked her what's wrong?'

'I tried, but I didn't get anywhere. I got the feeling she doesn't want to talk to me.'

'If you want to see her again, you'll have to find some way of getting her to explain what's going on, won't you? Perhaps you could write her a letter? Tell her that you care for her and you don't understand what you might have done to upset her.'

'I'll think about it. She'd probably just tear it up.'

'She might... There's always that chance, but you won't know unless you try, will you?'

Alex laughed softly. 'You're good to me, Jen. You're always trying to pep me up, aren't you?'

Some of his friends were making a move to leave, and he said, 'I should go and say goodbye to them.'

It was already well past midnight, Jenna realised with a sense of shock, and she ought to start thinking of making the journey back. She was glad the week-end was coming up and she didn't have to be up early in the morning.

'I'd better think about going as well,' she murmured.

He frowned. 'You'll stay here tonight, won't you, Jen?'

'Well...I don't know about that...I thought I'd head for home.'

He shook his head. 'The wind's getting up outside, and the sea will be too choppy on the way back. Besides, there's no need to make all that effort when there's a spare bedroom here that you can use.'

Just thinking about braving the water and the cold wind made her feel like shivering. Added to that, the recent late nights were beginning to catch up with her and the enticement of a warm bed here meant that there was no contest at all.

Jenna gave in. 'OK. You win. Show me the way.'

They decided to leave the clearing up until the next morning, though Jenna stacked what she could into the dishwasher and moved most of the debris into the kitchen.

When she finally went upstairs to bed, she took off her skirt and top and slid under the duvet in her underwear. The bed was soft and enveloping, blissfully comfortable, and it wasn't long before she fell into a deep sleep.

She dreamed she was lying on a sun-kissed beach, where the waves gently rolled in and broke on the shore in lacy ribbons of foam. The sun warmed her skin, and she was totally relaxed, not wanting to move.

Then Alex came to stand beside her, urging her to get up.

'Not yet,' she murmured sleepily. 'It's heavenly

here. Bliss.' The warm sand heated her skin, and she stretched lazily, her bare arm sweeping languidly over the duvet.

But he wasn't taking no for an answer. 'I've brought you some tea,' he said, and she smiled, sinking further into her pillow as she turned onto her side.

'Thanks,' she mumbled drowsily. 'You're a lovely man.'

'Am I?' he said, and the voice was huskily amused now, although there was also a new, subtle timbre that didn't quite add up. She frowned a little, hazily wondering what it was that had changed.

The warm, sandy beach of her dreams called softly to her again, though, and she curled her toes into the softness of her duvet and sighed happily. 'Lovely golden sand,' she murmured.

'Is it?'

The lightly voiced question roused her once more, and slowly she blinked again, trying to fend off the mists of sleep and focus properly. She looked up and her gaze meshed with vivid blue eyes, as blue as the hot azure sky of her dream.

'Hello, sleepyhead,' Ross said. 'Can I join you, wherever you are?'

CHAPTER SIX

THERE must be something wrong with her vision. That had to be it. Jenna rubbed her eyes with her knuckles and struggled to concentrate her attention on the man at the side of the bed.

Her gaze shifted over him. He was all too familiar, tall and muscular, his body fit and lithe, his mouth quirked into a wry grin. It was Ross standing there, sure enough.

She closed her eyes briefly, then opened them again to make sure that she hadn't been imagining things. But she really wasn't dreaming any longer.

Her heart started to thump erratically as realisation set in, and she made to sit up in the bed, before suddenly remembering that she was clad only in a silky camisole and briefs. Warm colour flooded her cheeks and she fumbled for the duvet which had slipped down, clutching it to her with a bare arm.

'Modesty, Jenna? Why are you trying to hide away from me?' He sent her an intimate, teasing, blue glance. 'It's much too late for that, you know. I've already had a wonderfully tantalising glimpse of your deliciously feminine charms when you swept the duvet away in your sleep. You must have had some restless dreams, or perhaps you were simply too warm in the night.'

Her eyes widened in dismay, a small frown working its way into her brow. 'What are you doing here?' she managed huskily.

'I came over to see my brother. It's the weekend, remember? No work today, hopefully, so I came to help him with the farm.' He came and sat down on the edge of the bed beside her. 'I wasn't expecting to find you here.'

That worked both ways. 'I wasn't expecting to see you.'

'I gathered that.' A smile tugged at his mouth. 'You looked so beautifully startled. Soft and vulnerable, and helplessly feminine.'

Shakily, she pushed her fingers through the tumbled mass of her curls. 'I, um…I really wasn't thinking straight.'

'Weren't you?' His voice took on a low, sexy timbre. 'It's a shame you don't think straight more often when I'm around if that's going to be the result.' His eyes glinted with devilish flame and her gaze tangled with his, caught up in that smoky heat.

'What do you mean?' she asked in a breathless whisper, still doing battle with the realisation that he was actually here in the house.

Ross laughed softly, leaning forward so that she edged back into the softness of her pillows and looked up at him with wide, green eyes. 'Well,' he murmured, 'you do look so enticingly sweet and softly inviting…and you are in my bed after all.'

'*Your* bed?' Puzzled, she worked her way unsteadily through the filmy curtains of sleep that still clouded her thoughts. 'How can it be your bed?'

'This used to be my room, don't you remember? You've been in this house before so it can't be un-

familiar to you. It's been changed around a bit in the
last year or so...perhaps that's why you forgot. I still
use this room whenever I stay over.'

He was very close to her now, so that if she'd
reached out she might have touched him with the tips
of her fingers and registered his warmth. The faint
scent of his aftershave teased her nostrils, a very subtle fragrance of musk. She could feel the heat ema-
nating from him, and his nearness flustered her so that
she said quickly, 'I meant to say I didn't know whose
bed it was...'

'Didn't you? That's a great pity because, you
know, I think I could get used to having you here.'
He looked down into her confused face and gently
shifted position, lightly pressuring her backwards, a
hand placed at either side of her head, his body making searing contact with her own. As he moved, her
breasts were gently crushed against him, and hot sensation swept like liquid flame through her veins.

And then he brought his mouth down to capture
hers, and any words of husky protest that might have
formed in her throat were softly muffled. His lips
teased the ripe fullness of her own, coaxing her with
such sensual expertise that her entire body melted beneath his in startled response.

Blood surged dizzyingly in her head as his stroking
fingers discovered her softly feminine shape, and she
sighed raggedly as she felt the slow glide of his hand
at her waist, feathering down over her supple abdomen.

Jenna's body responded to him with a will all of
its own, moulding itself to his seductive embrace, her
fingers reaching up to explore the firm muscles of his

arms. She clung to him, compelled by the urgent demand of his mouth and hands to abandon all caution.

Ripples of unexpected pleasure quivered through her, leaving her limbs pliant, her body languid, and she gave a faint, shuddery sigh as his lips shifted, dipped down to trail over the silken column of her throat and linger on the velvet smoothness of her flesh. She savoured every sweet moment as he brushed kisses lightly over the sweep of her shoulders. Then his lips slid down to glide smoothly over the soft curve of her breasts.

'Ross...' A small gasp broke in her throat. It was almost too much to bear, this sweet, slow seduction. The blood sizzled in her veins as his seeking lips shifted to explore every contour of her body, and she moved sensually beneath him, revelling in his male power and gentle strength. Her skin was on fire where his lips and hands touched her, and she didn't know how much more of this she could take before she went beyond the point of all reason...

'What is it, sweetheart?'

'I...I'm not... I mean...all this is happening too fast for me,' she muttered unsteadily. 'I need time to think.' Her fingers tangled with his shirt, gently pushing him away, and he eased himself away from her with a soft groan.

Now that he was no longer holding her close, she felt suddenly bereft, but at least it helped to clear her head a little. This was Ross, her Ross, the only man she had ever loved, and she needed to know that it was right between them. She had always loved him, always wanted him, but why had he never said that he loved her? Why was he here now, making sweet love to her, when only a short time ago he'd been urging her to go after the job she wanted? Would he have done that, would he be sending her away if he really cared deeply about her? Wasn't the real truth the most painful thing in the world that she had to acknowledge—that, in fact, he didn't love her at all?

And what about Annie? Where did she belong in his life?

'Jenna?' It was a softly voiced question, and she looked up at him and tried not to see the banked embers of fire that glimmered in the depths of his eyes.

'I'm sorry, Ross...I think I need some time to sort out my feelings.'

'You're having second thoughts?' He raked a hand through his hair, his gaze fixed on her warily.

'Yes,' she whispered. 'I think I am.'

'But why? I thought you were with me all the way.'

'Maybe I was...but you came in here when I was half-asleep,' she said unevenly, 'and then you started kissing me, and it all got a bit confused after that.'

She wished things could be different, but he'd kissed her only because he'd found her in his bed, half-dressed, and it had been a purely physical, momentary arousal, nothing more. He didn't want anything but sensual enjoyment of her body—she didn't think he was looking to share any loving feelings she might have to offer.

He said huskily, 'This is all about Alex really, isn't it?'

The blunt question startled her. Her eyes grew large. 'Why would you think that? Alex has nothing to do with this.'

He shook his head. 'I don't believe you. I've

thought for a long time that you were more than just fond of him, and perhaps I should have realised that it went deeper than that when you came over here to be with him last night.'

'You've got it all wrong—'

'I don't think so.' His mouth hardened. 'He's a very relevant part of this equation—you were so concerned about propriety when I suggested that you might come to live at the surgery, but that argument all falls down when it comes to staying here with Alex, doesn't it?'

'That's because the two situations are very different,' she said quickly. 'This is your mother's house, for one thing, and I've only spent one night here.' She frowned. 'And that was only because it was too difficult for me to get home. You shouldn't be accusing me of having an ulterior motive.'

'I wasn't accusing you of anything,' he returned crisply. 'But if you're pinning your hopes on Alex, I think you're wasting your time. As it is, he's hopelessly distracted these days. It's more than time he knuckled down to some serious work and got his career on track, and the last thing he needs is a complicated emotional attachment with you.'

'So suddenly I'm to blame for everything that's wrong in Alex's life, am I?' Her temper rose like a heat haze. 'And just because you think we shouldn't be close, I'm the one who has to make the changes? Think again, Ross. It isn't going to happen. Alex may well have one or two weaknesses, but I like your brother a lot, I care about what goes on in his life, and if he needs my support I'll be there for him, no matter what objections you might have. I'm not going to conveniently fade into the background.'

'If you're holding out the hope that he'll change his ways for you, you're wasting your time. He's irresponsible, and happy-go-lucky, and around you he'll never have any reason to change. He can't match you so he won't even try. You're the strong one. And you'll come to realise one day that you'll only be happy with someone who's equally strong.'

'And who might that be?'

He threw her a lancing stare. 'I'm sure he'll turn up one day, when you've made up your mind what it is that you want from life.'

'As if I haven't already?'

'You just think you have. There's too much going on for you to settle to anything yet.'

Jenna tossed him an emerald glare. 'I've already made up my mind about one thing…'

'What's that?'

'I want you to go. Now—so that I can get dressed.'

His mouth twisted. 'As you please.' He shrugged dismissively. 'When you're ready to come downstairs there will be some breakfast waiting and fresh tea in the pot.' His glance went to the bedside table. 'I expect the cup I brought you has gone cold by now.'

As he turned on his heel and walked calmly to the door, she scowled at the cup and felt like throwing it at him.

Alex was in the kitchen when she went in there a few minutes later. He looked pleased to see her, and she smiled back at him, ignoring Ross, whose gaze narrowed on her from over the newspaper he was reading. As she sat down at the table, he folded the paper and put it to one side.

'Help yourself, Jen,' Alex said. 'There's cereal and toast, and some of Mum's home-made marmalade if you want it, too. Oh, and grapefruit as well.'

He was pouring tea from the big china pot and offered her a cup. 'I'm sorry I wasn't here first thing this morning. I was called away to go and help Tom get Steve to the ferry. You were sound asleep, and I didn't want to wake you.'

'That's all right.' She sprinkled sugar onto a fresh grapefruit and dipped a spoon into the fruit. 'How is he today?'

'Subdued. A bit depressed, I'd say, but that probably follows after the stuff he took, doesn't it? He certainly doesn't remember anything that happened last night.'

'I didn't think he would.' She was aware of Ross's speculative gaze, but she avoided returning it, and steadfastly carried on eating.

She was on her second round of toast when Ross's phone bleeped insistently, and she heard his tone change to one of immediate concern as he spoke to whoever was on the line.

'When did this happen? Yes, of course you did the right thing. Just loosen any of her clothing which might be hindering her breathing and make her as comfortable as you can. I'll be right over.'

Jenna glanced across at him, and saw that he'd paled. Getting to his feet, he said to Alex, 'It's Mum, she's had some sort of collapse. It sounds as though it might be serious. I'm going to go over there now and find out what's happened.'

He was halfway to the door already. 'I'll come with you,' Jenna said, and hoped he wouldn't argue. This was no time to carry on a personal feud, when his mother's health might be at stake, and she desperately wanted to do what she could to help. Flora had always treated her as though she'd been her own daughter.

'OK. Let's go.'

'What about me?' Alex said. 'Can I do anything to help?'

'You'd probably do best to stay here and collect a few things for her, nightclothes and toiletries, just in case,' Ross said quickly. 'I'll let you know what's happening.'

'All right. I suppose it might only make her anxious if we all turn up.'

They ran to the quay, and Ross threw the boat into top speed, so that they hurtled across the water. Jenna held onto the rail and was thankful that the sea was relatively calm now.

They picked up his car at the far quay, and drove the rest of the way as fast as he dared. By the time they arrived at the house where Flora had been staying with her friend, Jenna was feeling windswept and slightly nauseous with anxiety. She hurried inside, wanting to see for herself Flora's condition.

'She just went all faint…and she couldn't get her breath,' Jeannie MacDonald said, looking flustered and distressed at the same time. 'I didn't know what to do.'

She started to walk along the hall, moving awkwardly and bending over a little as though she was in pain, and Jenna thought that her kidney infection must still be giving her trouble.

Jeannie ushered them through to the kitchen, where Flora was lying half-slumped on the floor, but with her head supported by cushions. 'She fell and I wasn't able to lift her. I know she must have hurt herself, she went down with such a bang. I thought she'd knocked herself out, but her eyes are open. I've been so worried about her. Can you do something?'

Ross hurried over to Flora, kneeling down beside her and saying gently, 'It's all right, Mum, I'm here, and Jenna's with me. We'll make you feel more comfortable.'

He checked her breathing and listened to her heart, and Jenna put an arm around Jeannie and led her out into the hall. She wanted to keep her away while Ross tended to his mother. At this time, Flora needed to be kept calm.

'We'll look after her, Jeannie. Do you think you could find a blanket, or something that we can cover her with?' she murmured. 'It will help if we can keep her warm.'

'Oh, yes… Yes, I'll go and find one now.' She looked back towards the kitchen, her face drawn with lines of worry and her cheekbones flushed with fever. 'She will be all right, won't she? You will be able to do something for her?'

'We'll take care of her, I promise. Just try and keep calm, Jeannie, and don't rush about. You've not been well yourself, have you?'

Jenna was anxious to get back to Flora, but she knew Ross would do everything he could to help his mother, and at the moment it was important to keep Jeannie occupied to keep her from flapping and making Flora more anxious than she must already be. It wasn't likely that she would be content to sit quietly in a chair and rest.

She spoke gently to Jeannie, persuading her to fetch the blanket from the ottoman in the bedroom, and then to collect up Flora's things and put them in her overnight case. Jeannie seemed glad to have something specific to do, and while she was occupied Jenna went back into the kitchen.

She knelt down beside Ross, and covered Flora with the blanket. She looked dreadfully ill, and it was terribly upsetting to see her like that.

Ross was giving his mother oxygen. 'Her heart rhythm's chaotic, very rapid,' he said in a tone so low that Jenna didn't think Flora could have heard him.

'I've given her an anticoagulant and something to regulate the heartbeat, but we need to get her to hospital.' Without an anticoagulant, the risk was that she might suffer a stroke, and they wanted to avoid that at all costs.

Jenna nodded and helped out with the oxygen while Ross moved away to call for the ambulance. Flora had always hated the thought of going to hospital, probably because she was usually such a self-confident, motivated individual, and in hospital you were sick and vulnerable. Seeing the stricken look in Flora's eyes, Jenna reached out to gently stroke her hand.

'You'll be more comfortable there,' she told her in a soothing tone, 'and Ross will go with you, so you've no need to worry.' She glanced down and saw that he'd splinted the wrist that Flora had fallen on. She asked, 'Are you in any pain?'

Flora managed to shake her head slightly, and

Jenna thought that Ross must have given her an injection that would give her some relief. What Flora needed now, more than anything, was reassurance.

When Jeannie came into the room and saw that her friend was still desperately ill, she started to panic all over again.

'It's my fault this has happened,' she said tearfully. 'She looked so exhausted before she collapsed. I feel so guilty. She must have tired herself out, looking after me. I should never have let her come here.'

'You mustn't blame yourself,' Ross said quietly, drawing her to one side. 'She may have an underlying heart problem that has caused it to suddenly race. We weren't able to detect it until now, but that's probably the reason she felt faint, and it probably accounts for the falls she's been having recently.'

The ambulance came within a few minutes, and Jenna watched as Ross spoke in a low voice to the paramedics, before walking alongside his mother's stretcher and climbing into the back of the vehicle. He would be there with her on the long journey to the hospital, making sure that she was being monitored every step of the way, and that must surely be a comfort to her.

'I'll let Alex know what's happening,' Jenna said. 'You'll keep in touch, won't you?'

'I'll phone you,' Ross answered, his features shadowed as the doors began to close on him.

Jenna's eyes blurred with tears as the ambulance drew away. Sometimes it was so hard to have to stand back and do nothing, but leave everything in other people's hands. She dashed away the wetness with the back of her hand and turned back to Jeannie.

'Perhaps we should go inside and put the kettle on,' she said huskily, 'and you can tell me how you've been managing over the last few days. Are your tablets helping to make you feel any better? I ought to take your temperature while I'm here, just to see how you're doing.'

She stayed with Jeannie for a while, settling her as best she could. When she was satisfied that the medication was doing its job, and that Jeannie was going to rest and drink plenty of fluids, she made her way back to the cottage and phoned Alex, who must be worried sick.

After that, there was nothing she could do but wait until she had more news.

Ross stayed at the hospital the whole of that day and the next, confirming with Jenna that she would hold the fort in his absence. There was little change in Flora's condition, but she wasn't any worse, which was something.

He said that he'd been to look in on Kirsty while he was there. 'She's sitting up now, and taking notice of what's going on around her. She doesn't remember an awful lot about what happened that day, except that she wanted to go to the farm with Connor.'

'Perhaps it's just as well,' Jenna said.

At least Jenna could keep herself busy through the long hours of waiting. The men were coming to fit a new cooker in her kitchen on Monday morning, and she spent most of Sunday fixing tiles to the back wall in readiness.

Ross arrived back at the surgery on Monday morning, having stayed a second night at the hospital. His features were strained, and there were shadows under his eyes, probably a legacy from lack of sleep. A hint of dark stubble showed that he needed a shave.

A wave of compassion welled up inside Jenna, and she wanted to reach out and touch his arm, to show him that she cared. But the memory of what had happened between them on Saturday morning held her back.

He moved briskly to the stairs, throwing back as he went, 'Apologise to everyone for me being late, will you? I want to go and freshen up ready for surgery. I won't be more than a few minutes.'

Jenna watched his departing figure with a frown. Clearly, she was going to have to wait until after her morning clinic before she would have the chance to speak to him.

She was doing the child health checks this morning, part of the immunisation programme, and there were about a dozen mums and their babies or toddlers waiting already.

She said a friendly 'Good morning,' to them as she went to her room, then called for her first little patient.

Halfway through the morning she went to Reception to collect the next batch of notes and grab a cup of coffee, and met up with Ross there. He was checking blood-test results that had come in the post, and he looked up as she passed by him.

'Thank you for helping me to look after my mother and for taking care of things here while I was away,' he said quietly. 'Everything was so rushed and urgent that I didn't have a chance to tell you how grateful I am for all that you did.'

'You don't need to thank me. I think of Flora as

my own family,' Jenna answered softly. 'Has there been any improvement?'

'Her heart rate hasn't settled down yet, so they're doing what they can to regulate it, and they're continuing with the anticoagulant therapy. She needs to rest, but she's feeling very anxious, of course.'

He glanced through the glass partition to the waiting room. 'Mums and toddlers today. I expect you're in your element.'

He was changing the subject to something less painful, and she nodded, murmuring, 'I think you must be right about the birth rate going up—there's quite a crowd out there.'

As she spoke, someone came up to the partition to speak to Mairi, and Jenna recognised that it was Annie. She was a pretty girl, with glossy chestnut curls and a lively face, a peaches-and-cream complexion.

'Is Ross here this morning?' Annie said. Then, looking into the office area beyond, her face lit up and she added, 'Oh, yes, there he is. I wonder if he'll see me now?'

Ross waved a hand towards her, indicating for her to go to the side door, and went around to meet her. 'Hello, Annie. It's good to see you.' He draped an arm around her shoulders, his mouth curving in a smile.

'And you. I didn't know you were going to be away for the whole weekend. I really wanted to ask you how Flora is,' she said. 'It all happened so suddenly, didn't it? It must have been a terrible shock.'

Ross nodded, drawing her away towards his room,

and Jenna heard him say, 'It was. Come in here and we can talk. Are you OK?'

'I'm fine, apart from this insect bite on my leg that's giving me some trouble. Perhaps you could have a look at it while I'm here?'

Jenna watched them move off and saw the door to his surgery close firmly on the two of them. She didn't stay to see how long they were closeted to-gether in the privacy of his room. She didn't think she wanted to know and instead of waiting around, she picked up her coffee cup and went back to work.

CHAPTER SEVEN

THE pace was hectic in the days that followed, and Jenna didn't see all that much of Ross. The weather had changed for the better, and along with it came a rising number of tourists, who wanted to take advantage of the sunshine. It meant that Ross was out on call far more often than usual, dealing with the various scrapes that they got themselves into.

She missed him. She didn't want to admit that to herself, but it was a fact and it was something she was going to have to get used to all over again when the time came for her to leave the island. In a few weeks, when the new doctor came to work with Ross, there would be no place for Jenna here.

Over the week, when she had the chance, she went to see Flora in hospital and tried to comfort her and cheer her up as best she could. The rest of the time, when she wasn't seeing friends, she set to work on her refurbished kitchen. The renovations were almost complete, and she was pleased with the results.

Ross came by on Saturday morning when she was weeding the flower beds at the back of the house. He looked as though he was in a hurry and she knew straight away that this wasn't just a friendly social visit.

'I've just had a call from the Quayside Hotel,' he told her briskly. 'A woman's gone into premature labour, from the sound of things. Her waters have broken. She's a diabetic, on insulin. I've got everything we'll need, so do you want to come along?'

'Yes, please.' She threw him a quick smile. 'You know I would.'

'Good. I thought you might actually want to take over on this one. Apart from it being more your field, the mother might feel better having a woman in charge of things.'

Jenna knew that, in fact, he was more than capable when it came to handling obstetric cases, even difficult ones, and in asking her to do this he was considering the pregnant woman's feelings above all. It was typical of him, and it made her heart warm to acknowledge that. A small part of her was pleased as well that he was putting complete trust in her.

'I'll be right with you,' she said, gathering up the trowel and fork she'd been using and pushing them hastily into a box in the shed. Whipping off her gardening gloves, she added, 'Just give me a minute to wash my hands and change into some fresh clothes.'

A few minutes later she was reaching for her medical bag and they were on their way.

'She's about four weeks early,' Ross told her on the drive to the hotel. 'She and her husband are here for a weekend break, a last holiday before the birth, by all accounts. The husband thinks his wife has been overdoing things in the last few weeks, getting ready for the birth, and that might have started her off. Either that, or the upheaval of coming away.'

'Is it a first pregnancy, do you know?'

He shook his head. 'Second. They've a little girl, about two years old. She's with them, but the hotel people have arranged for someone to look after her.'

'That will probably be a relief for them.'

The hotel manager hurried to meet them in the foyer. 'Thanks for coming, Ross...and you, too, Jenna. I'm glad you could make it—the lass is getting a bit anxious, as you might expect. We've moved her to a room where she can be a bit more peaceful—there's less coming and going in that wing of the building, and we've done what we can to make her comfortable.'

'That was good of you,' Ross murmured. 'She'll probably appreciate that when she has time to stop and think about it.'

'Och, it was nae bother. You'll let us know if there's anything you need, will you?'

'We will.'

He ushered them into the lift up to the first floor. 'Your brother was in here earlier,' he told Ross. 'He was having a drink with a friend, and chatting with some of our guests.'

He turned to Jenna. 'I thought I heard him say that he was going to look for you, but I expect he'll catch up with you later.'

'Did he? I shouldn't imagine it was anything too urgent,' Jenna murmured, conscious of Ross's pene-trating glance. She wasn't going to let his irrational concerns throw her. If he believed she was in love with Alex, that was his problem, not hers.

The woman, Debbie, was lying on the bed in her room, looking pale and distracted and clearly in some pain. Her husband stood nervously by her side, white-faced, not knowing what to do, and obviously panic-stricken by the unexpected event.

'Is she going to be all right?' he asked as soon as
Jenna came up to them and introduced herself.

'Of course she is,' she answered with a smile,
glancing at Debbie to see how she was coping. There
was a film of sweat on her brow, and in another minute or so she suddenly tensed as another strong contraction of the uterus took hold.

'Try to relax, Debbie,' Jenna murmured. 'Concentrate on your breathing. That's right—soft, small
breaths. That's lovely. I'll have a quick a look at you
and make sure that all is well.'

Ross took the husband to one side to confirm any
of the medical history which might have been left out
during their phone call and to make sure that they had
everything they needed to prepare for the birth.

After a swift examination, Jenna confirmed that
Debbie was definitely about to give birth. 'You're
fully dilated,' she told her, 'so it shouldn't be long
now. Would you like me to give you a shot of something to help ease the pain?'

Debbie nodded, and the relief showed on her face
when Jenna had administered the injection and it
gradually started to take effect.

Jenna turned her attention to checking the baby's
heartbeat with a foetal stethoscope. It sounded reas-
suringly steady.

Ross said, 'I'll see if I can get the manager to rustle
up a baby bath or laundry basket to put the baby in
when it's born.' He grinned. 'That's the only thing
that seems to be missing, as far as I can tell.' He
phoned Reception to arrange it, then came back to the
bedside.

'How have you been managing your diabetes?' he

asked, as he wrapped a cuff around Debbie's arm and took a blood-pressure reading. 'Have you been maintaining your blood-glucose levels?'

Debbie nodded. 'The obstetrician back home said it was important. He said it was possible the baby might be too big if I didn't.'

That might be a problem, but Jenna was keeping her fingers crossed that they were in luck with this one. From her examination she thought that Debbie's baby could probably be delivered normally.

Another contraction swept over Debbie just then, and she squeezed her husband's hand tightly. 'Oh, it's coming,' she said breathlessly. 'I can feel it coming.'

The contraction subsided after a while, and Jenna said, 'Don't push any more, Debbie. Wait till you have another one.' She gave her a local anaesthetic and made an episiotomy to prevent the tissues from tearing when the head emerged.

A few minutes later, as the walls of the uterus contracted again, she said, 'Now, Debbie, push hard...that's the way, a good strong push, as hard as you can.'

In the next breath she said, 'I can see the head coming. That's great, you're doing fine...wonderful. It's through...the head's through, Debbie. Well done...' She looked up and smiled. 'That's the worst bit over.'

A shoulder appeared next, then the other, then the whole of the infant emerged, and Jenna laughed suddenly with the release of pent-up emotion, a softly joyful laugh that mingled with the squall of protest from the baby who had struggled into the world.

'It's a girl,' Ross said, his mouth curving as Jenna

lifted the infant onto the mother's abdomen. 'She's perfect, she's beautiful.'

Jenna quickly wiped the baby's face, while Ross clamped the cord and cut it. Then she wrapped the newborn snugly in a blanket and handed her into Debbie's waiting arms.

'Isn't she gorgeous?' Jenna looked at Ross, over-come, her eyes brimming with emotion, and he put his arms around her and hugged her.

'Isn't she?' he said, 'and it was such an easy de-livery, too. I can hardly believe it.'

Jenna hugged him back. 'They both look as though they're doing just fine, don't they?'

Debbie was crying and laughing, at the same time, but after a few minutes she sobered a little.

'Another girl, John,' she said softly, looking up at her husband, a tiny worry line cutting into her brow. 'Do you mind very much?'

'Why would I mind?' John said with a dazed ex-pression on his face. He reached out to touch the in-fant's little hand, and grinned as her tiny fist curled around his finger. 'She's absolutely lovely. And she's so small, isn't she, when we were expecting her to be huge?'

Jenna smiled at that. The baby still had to be weighed, but she suspected that she would be some-thing around six pounds.

She dealt with the other tasks that were left—de-livering the placenta, checking the mother's condi-tion—while Ross took care of the new arrival, weigh-ing her and going through all the procedures of neonatal care.

They left the couple alone with the baby some half

an hour later, and as they walked to the lift Jenna said in an awed tone, 'That was so exhilarating, wasn't it? I don't think I'll ever experience anything more wonderful than seeing a baby being born.'

'Or me,' Ross said with a smile.

'I'm still walking on clouds,' she murmured, her heart singing. 'It's not every day I see a new life into the world... I don't feel like going back home yet, do you? It would be too mundane and out of place on a day like today, don't you think?'

'I know what you mean. We should celebrate.' He grinned. 'Shall we stay and have a late lunch here in the hotel? They've built a new terrace restaurant where you can look out over the bay while you eat. Besides, it will give me a chance to thank you properly for everything you've done to help me out just lately. I've been wanting to do that for some time now, but we never did get around to having that picnic on the beach, did we, with my mother suddenly being taken ill?'

'I told you before, you don't have to thank me,' Jenna said her mouth curving. 'I should like to have lunch on the terrace, though. It sounds perfect.'

'That's what we'll do, then...and maybe we could go for a walk along the beach afterwards.'

'That sounds lovely. I'd like that. It's such a warm, sunny day that it seems a shame to be indoors.'

They made their way up to the restaurant on the second floor, and she said wistfully, 'I wish there was better news about Flora. The last time I saw her she wanted to come out of hospital, but the doctors were still worried about her heart rate not settling down.'

'She is improving, though. I spoke to them this

morning, and they were a bit more optimistic. She doesn't need the oxygen as much now.'

'That's good news. I'm glad.' She was pensive for a moment or two. 'What will you do when she comes out of hospital? She won't be able to manage on her own.'

'No, she won't.' Ross rested the flat of his hand on the curve of Jenna's lower back as he guided her along the plushly carpeted corridor towards the restaurant, and she tried not to let it distract her. 'I'll have to give it some thought. I might at some stage go back to live in the house myself, but that won't be a complete answer, of course.'

'And it would mean you'd have to cross the water to get to the surgery every day.'

'That's no major problem. As it is, I have to travel around three islands to do my job.'

'That's true enough. At least you've a cabin cruiser to keep the worst of the weather off.'

Jenna was stunned by her first sight of the newly built restaurant. One wall was made almost entirely of glass, giving a panoramic view over the bay, and glass doors opened onto a paved terrace beyond, where people sat and talked over drinks.

They chose a table by the window where they could eat and watch the breakers roll in from the Atlantic. In the distance they could see puffins congregating on the rocks. Nearer to where they were, gulls swooped down over the harbour, looking for titbits where fishermen hauled in their nets.

Jenna dipped her fork into her salad and ate slowly, with enjoyment, happy to see the tourists walking along the quayside with their children dancing along in front of them, revelling in the sunshine.

'They look so carefree, don't they, the little ones?'

Ross studied her thoughtfully, his eyes darkening, then said quietly, 'Have you ever thought about having children of your own?'

'Oh…I've thought about it, yes. I do want children of my own one day. It's just that I can't imagine it happening yet.'

'Because you're still trying to get your career together?'

'I suppose that's it. I seem to have been on the move over the last few years, but perhaps when things are more settled I'll be able to think about it more seriously.'

There had been men friends, of course, but no one she'd ever wanted to spend the rest of her life with. The trouble was, she thought with a wry inner smile, she always found herself comparing them to Ross, and that meant that they always fell short of her ideal.

As to Ross himself, he would never be without girlfriends. Women mostly found him irresistible, herself included. It was a forlorn hope, though, that he would even think of her in a purely romantic way.

True enough, he'd kissed her, he'd made her feel for a time as though she'd been floating on air, but it hadn't meant anything to him.

He was frowning now, but he said gently enough, 'You've plenty of time yet.' It was as though, without needing any explanations, he understood her misgivings about leaving motherhood too late. She nodded, and hoped he would never be able to read her thoughts regarding him.

Her relationship with Ross was a very special one, she recognised that. He would always be her best friend and he would always look out for her, but that was only because he felt protective towards her, probably a legacy from their childhood.

They had drinks on the terrace after their meal, and he told her how he and Alex would often come here to the hotel to relax for a time whenever his brother was back home.

'He likes the island,' he said, 'but I'm not sure it has the pull for him that you might expect. He's always looked further afield, thinking that the grass is greener on the other side of the fence. I suppose he'll make up his mind what he wants eventually.'

Some half an hour later they made their way down to the beach. Jenna slipped off her sandals and carried them, letting her toes sink into the warm sand.

She was wearing a skimpy ribbed top and a loose, flowing skirt, and it was good to feel the light breeze around her limbs as she walked. Ross took off his shoes and socks, and held her hand as they headed towards a large boat that was pulled up near the water's edge.

Kirsty's grandfather, James, was there, helping tourists into the boat, getting ready for an excursion out to sea. He stopped and waved to them as they drew near, and Ross asked, 'Is there any more news of Kirsty?'

'Aye. They'll be keeping her in hospital for another day or so. She had a lung infection that kept her temperature up a bit, but she's getting better now.' He smiled. 'She's well enough to keep the nurses on their toes, at any rate.'

'That's good,' Ross said with a laugh. 'Let me know as soon as she comes home, and I'll come over to see her.'

They moved on further along the beach, and Jenna paddled at the water's edge, kicking up her feet and splashing Ross when he threatened to pick her up and toss her in. In the scramble her skirt was soaked, and she lifted it up and wrinkled her nose, telling him, 'Now look what you did!'

Ross wasn't looking at her skirt, though. He scanned her long legs appreciatively, his blue eyes glinting, the colour of the sea.

'Time was when you practically lived in jeans and there was never a sight of bare flesh. Nowadays, look at you—you're flaunting it right, left and centre.'

Jenna arched a delicate brow, a mocking smile playing around her lips. 'Are you complaining about the way I choose to dress? You might well be a few years older than I am, and that might just possibly have given you a say in things a few years back, but that time is well and truly over. I'm a grown woman now and, I'm warning you, I shall do exactly as I please.'

'I'd noticed,' he said in a lazy drawl. 'Just watch out that the big, bad wolf doesn't get you…'

'And what's that supposed to mean?'

'Don't you know anything?' He shook his head, and she ought to have been warned by the stealthy way he'd crept closer, without her realising that he'd even moved, that he was up to something.

In the next second he'd grabbed her round the waist and tussled her to the ground. She fought him off, laughing and slapping at his chest with the flat of her hands as he growled and nuzzled at her throat.

'Too late,' he said. 'You're done for now.'

What might have happened next she never found out, because a shadow loomed over them and Alex said cheerfully, 'So there you are. I've been looking all over for you.'

Jenna blinked and looked up, shielding her eyes from the sun, and would have smiled, except that she was suddenly aware of the tension in Ross's body. He let go of her and rose to his feet in one fluid movement, a frown darkening his features.

Alex squared up to him and said in a mock-threatening tone, 'Have you quite finished messing with my girl? I need to talk to her.'

Ross threw him a scowl in return and muttered something under his breath that Jenna didn't catch. Alex coloured momentarily, then laughed and held out a hand to her, pulling her to her feet.

She gave him a quick, affectionate hug, conscious all the time of Ross's brooding presence. The two men had been kidding around, a brotherly spat grounded in male ego, but there were undercurrents going on here, and she wondered fleetingly why Ross's mood had changed for the worse since Alex had come on the scene.

Bemused, she tried to smooth down her skirt, now wet and covered with sand. 'I heard you'd been looking for me,' she said huskily to Alex, trying to collect her wits. 'What's so important? There's nothing wrong, is there?'

'Nothing at all, only I was talking to some people at the hotel this morning and they said they'd been up to MacInnes Bluff and had seen the cottage. They've been up there before when it was empty, and thought what a good position it was in, overlooking the bay.'

He started to help her brush the sand off her skirt, and Ross observed them both for a moment in silence before going to search for their shoes which had become lost in the scuffle.

'Apparently, they've been coming to the island for holidays year after year,' Alex said, 'and now that they are about ready to retire they're thinking of settling here. They could see that a lot of improvements had been made to the cottage, and they wanted to know if it was likely to be put up for sale.'

He shrugged slightly, as though he was uncertain what he should have done. 'I said I wasn't sure what your plans were, but you might be open to offers.'

Ross had found their scattered shoes by now, and the three of them started to walk back along the beach the way they'd come.

'Did I do wrong in telling them that?' Alex sent her an enquiring look, as though he felt her silence might be a criticism of him.

'No...of course you didn't.' She hurried to reassure him, and tried to get her thoughts together. 'I know I should be making up my mind what I plan to do with the cottage in the end, but I've been putting it off and concentrating on getting it into a reasonable condition.'

'You won't be here to live in it, though, will you, if you go back to Perth? Even if this job at the centre falls through, you've other offers to consider over there, haven't you? After all, there's nothing for you here on the island, is there?'

She shook her head, and he went on, 'Ross made the appointment for the job at his practice when you were fixed up at the centre, and Dr Bartholomew is all set to come over here with her husband and two young children. They're going to live near Aisleen across the bay.'

'Are they? I didn't know that.' Jenna looked at Ross for confirmation, and he nodded.

'The house fell empty a couple of months back, and they put in an offer straight away.'

'That's turned out well for them.' Jenna was deep in thought as they approached the steps to the quay. Alex was right—it was getting close to the time when she ought to make a decision one way or the other.

'You could rent out the cottage through the summer,' Alex was saying, 'but it would probably be empty through the winter, and that's when it's likely to need more attention. You might end up having problems to deal with at the beginning of every season unless you hire someone to look after it for you.'

'That's true...but my father was thinking of letting it out, wasn't he?' She glanced up at Ross. 'Isn't that what you said?'

'He was, but he was here and able to keep an eye on it. He wouldn't have expected you to do the same.'

'Wouldn't he? What makes you think that?'

'He more or less told me so. He thought the world of you, and he wanted you to do what you felt was right, without having anyone else put pressure on you. He was proud of you, of the way you'd mapped out a career for yourself, and he didn't want anything to stand in your way. He asked me to look out for you, to make sure that nothing would stand in the way of your happiness.'

Jenna felt a lump come into her throat. 'That sounds as though he knew he was going to be ill. Did he have a premonition of some kind?'

Ross shook his head. 'I don't think so. I think he simply wanted to cover all eventualities.'

Somehow it made her feel good to know that her father had chosen Ross to confide in. It showed that her father had recognised Ross's strength of character and that he'd trusted him.

She said, 'I'm still not sure that I'm ready to make a decision either way. I know the sensible thing would be to sell up, but the house has been in my family for generations and I would feel as though I was losing something very precious if I were to let it go.'

And it would be so final, a severing of her links with the island if she sold her home here. She didn't think she was ready for that just yet.

'Perhaps you'll feel more sure of yourself when you know definitely about the job,' Alex said. 'You can't make plans when you don't know for certain where you'll be working, and if you miss out on this job and decide to take another, it would mean moving house in Perth. At the moment your flat is close to the health centre, but you might want to change that.'

He chuckled. 'One thing's for sure...you wouldn't need to worry about where to stay on the island if you sold up because there's always a place for you at Mum's.'

'You think of everything, don't you?' She smiled

at him, and then realised that they'd arrived back at the hotel where Ross's car was parked.

'I'll take you home,' Ross offered, 'unless you planned on staying here for a while longer?'

'Home will be fine.' Jenna glanced at Alex. 'Do you want to come over to the cottage?'

He nodded. 'I'd like that.'

When they arrived there, she said, 'You'll both come in for a coffee, won't you? I can show you the changes I've made.'

'I've been wanting to take another look,' Alex said, climbing out of the car and letting his glance wander over the freshly painted walls of the house and the pretty front garden. 'You've done well in the few weeks you've been here,' he commented. 'No wonder the visitors are asking about it.'

She looked at Ross, and for a moment he hesitated, frowning a little as he watched Alex walk up to the front door. Then he shook his head, saying, 'I should get back to the surgery. I've some work to clear up, and I'm supposed to be meeting Annie at six.'

'Oh...well, that's fine.' She tried not to let her disappointment show. 'I'll see you later, then.'

He left a short time later, and Alex followed her into the cottage, looking around and admiring her handiwork, the new cooker and the fireplace she'd had built in the sitting room.

'You've done wonders here.'

'Thanks. It's been hard work, but it was worth it, I think, in the end.' She glanced at him and saw an odd look come into his eyes, as though his mind had wandered off somewhere else.

'What are you thinking?' she asked quietly. 'Is

something wrong? You looked far away for a minute there.'

He pulled a face. 'It's probably time for me to start sorting my life out. I should find a place of my own someday soon...instead of just renting a house, I mean.'

'Why now? What's made you think about it now? Is it this girl that you were telling me about?'

'Rebecca? Yes, I think that must be it. She's made me re-evaluate things in a way, but I don't think I'm going to be making much headway with her.'

'You must be very keen on her if she's changing the way you think. Haven't you found out what went wrong yet?'

He shook his head. 'I've written to her, but I haven't had a reply. I think I'm going to have to go back to Perth and try and get her to at least talk to me.'

If he was planning on doing that, he must be smitten. Jenna had never known Alex go to such lengths. 'That's probably a good idea.'

He studied her quizzically. 'What about you and Ross? I interrupted something back there on the beach, didn't I?'

She shook her head. 'We were just fooling around. It didn't mean anything.'

'Didn't it? Aren't you in love with him?'

She stared at him, wide-eyed, before she collected herself.

'What makes you think that?'

'Just an instinct. I know you pretty well, Jen, and I get the feeling that you've loved him all your life, even if Ross is fool enough not to know it.'

She chewed at her lip. 'I should have known that I couldn't keep anything from you.' She was pensive for a moment. 'I hope he doesn't come to realise how I feel about him.' The thought that he might eventually guess made her feel incredibly nervous. 'It would be too humiliating to bear.'

'Why would it? How do you know he doesn't love you in return?'

She shook her head. 'He doesn't, Alex, I'm sure of it. He thinks this job on the mainland is the best thing that could happen to me, and he wants me to go for it. He wouldn't think that way if he loved me. Besides…there's Annie.'

Alex was silent for a moment. 'Yes, of course,' he said, 'there's Annie.'

CHAPTER EIGHT

Ross was later than usual coming down for surgery on Monday morning, and when he did eventually put in an appearance he looked as though he'd only just stepped out of the shower. His short, black hair gleamed like jet, spiky and glistening from the water, and he was still looping his tie and wriggling it into place as he dashed into Reception.

'Slow down,' Mairi instructed him. 'There are no patients in yet, so you've time for a coffee before you make a start. Have you had anything to eat?'

He shook his head. 'No time.' He ran his glance swiftly over his list for the morning. 'Dr Bartholomew's coming in for a look around this morning. I'll have to schedule the last patient for around eleven forty-five so that I'll be finished in time to meet her at twelve.'

He glanced at Jenna as he sifted through the post in his tray. 'You said you'd be able to do the home visits today—are you still OK with that?'

'It's fine by me,' Jenna murmured.

He made to head for his room, but Mairi stopped him. 'You should eat before you do anything,' she advised him sternly, 'or you'll be fit for nothing.' She turned to Jenna. 'Tell him, Jenna.'

Jenna rummaged in the cupboard and pulled out a packet of biscuits. 'Best I can do for the time being,' she said, tipping them out onto a plate and pushing it towards him. 'Were you called out?'

'No. Just a late night, and I overslept. I was trying to sort out what to do for the best when my mother comes out of hospital. I can't leave her to fend for herself, and Alex will be going back to Perth in another week or so.'

'Did you decide anything?' Jenna could understand how concerned he must be. 'If you want to arrange for someone to live in, to act as a kind of housekeeper and companion, I'll help out with the cost.'

He shook his head, and she said quickly, 'I meant what I said about Flora being like a mother to me. She was always there for me when I was growing up...and afterwards...and I want to do what I can for her. Aisleen said she heard that one of Flora's younger friends in the village was looking for a housekeeping place.'

Ross swallowed his coffee and bit into one of the biscuits. 'Thanks, Jenna, but I've managed to get it all sorted out. Mum will need someone who can help out with the farm, as well as keep an eye on her, and I think Annie's probably the best one to do that.'

'Annie?' She hadn't been expecting that.

He flipped open the office address book and ran a finger down the entries. 'She's qualified in farm management, and she gets on well with my mother, so we thought about arranging for her to live in.'

He frowned as he searched for a pen in his pocket. 'It was more or less a foregone conclusion that she would do that anyway. My mother thinks it's a good idea. She gets on well with Annie, so it's all just about settled. I'm going to help Annie to move in over the next day or so.' He wrote down an address on a slip of paper and pushed it into his jacket pocket.

Jenna tried to take in what he'd been saying. *More or less a foregone conclusion.* Was that what he'd had in mind the other day, when he'd said he might go and live at the house? She felt for a moment as though the breath had been knocked from her lungs. Perhaps Alex had been right all along when he'd quizzed Ross about a June wedding.

Her stomach made an uneasy somersault, churning painfully, but she was determined not to let him see how the news had affected her. She made a pretence of looking through her post while she waited for her insides to settle, but the letters might have been written in Chinese for all the sense she made of them.

Luckily, he was turning away, his mind fixed on gathering up the bundle of patients' notes, along with his coffee.

She mumbled, 'I'm glad you managed to work it all out, anyway.'

He smiled and nodded, busily munching on another biscuit. Then he headed off towards his room, and she pulled herself together and picked up her own batch of patients' notes.

Dr Bartholomew came into Reception at a quarter to twelve, when Jenna was in a corner of the office, looking through a hospital report. Jenna went over to meet her and introduced herself.

'So you're the doctor who's been working with Ross these last few weeks.' The woman smiled. 'I've heard such a lot about you, from Ross and from Aisleen at the shop in the village among others. Everyone thinks you've been doing a wonderful job.'

'That's nice to know. I'm sure you will, too.' She introduced her to Mairi, who'd been busy helping a patient to fill in a form. 'Ross is just seeing his last patient of the morning,' Jenna told her. 'He'll be along in a minute or two.'

'That's all right, I'm early. I've been over to the village to see the estate agent and make sure everything's in order for the move, and it all went without a hitch.' She laughed. 'It's not very often that things go through so smoothly, not where moving house is concerned, anyway. I can't wait to get settled here.'

'I'm sure you'll love it.' Jenna made her a coffee and asked about her family. She'd taken to Laura Bartholomew straight away. She had a friendly smile and a gentle way about her that would almost certainly endear her to the patients. Ross had made a good choice.

She tried not to think about what Laura's presence here meant, and how soon it would be before she herself wasn't needed.

Ross came to the reception area a couple of minutes later, and after they'd chatted for a while he whisked Laura off on a grand tour. She'd seen the place before, of course, but a lot of it must have passed over her head, and she was looking forward to taking it all in properly this time.

Jenna went out on a couple of home visits in the afternoon, and by the time she arrived back at the surgery Laura had left to catch the ferry with her family. Ross was talking to Annie, though, loading up his car with bits and pieces that Annie must have brought along with her, and they both gave Jenna a wave as she pulled her car into the empty parking slot.

'Ross is taking me over to the house so that I can start getting a few things organised,' Annie told her when Jenna had crossed the car park and met up with them. 'He picked a lot of my stuff up last night, ready to take over to the house, but I've just brought another couple of bags to add to the pile.'

She put her hands on her hips and surveyed the loaded boot. 'It will be good to have a day or so to get myself sorted before Flora comes home. I want to have the house spruced up a bit, because I don't suppose Alex will have bothered, and I thought I'd put some flowers about the place to welcome her back.'

'I'm sure she'll appreciate that,' Jenna said lightly. It was hard not to like Annie, but just at the moment it was a painful process to have to stand and talk to her as though her place in Ross's life didn't matter.

It hurt badly, a terrible ache in her solar plexus, to know that Annie was the one woman Ross cared about more than any other, and it was a pain that wouldn't simply ease with time.

'Do we know yet when she'll be coming home?' Jenna asked, glancing up at him.

'It looks as though it might be a couple of days,' he murmured. 'Of course, she wants it to be sooner, but the consultant wants to make sure that her readings are stable for a day or so before he'll risk letting her out. She'll stay on the anticoagulants for some time, and when she comes off those she'll need to take aspirin every day to keep her on form.'

'And a low-fat diet, I should imagine, if she's going to be prone to circulatory problems.'

'I'll see to it that she eats the right kind of food,' Annie said brightly. 'I like cooking, and it'll be great to have the run of that marvellous kitchen to try out my recipes.' She grinned at Ross. 'You've sampled my cooking, haven't you? What do you think of it?'

'I think you don't need to fish for compliments, Annie,' he said with a dry smile. 'You'll do very well.'

'Thank you for that.' She pushed a stack of books down into one corner. 'It'll help, having the produce from the farm to work with. Fresh fruit and vegetables, and free-range eggs.'

'I heard you'd done really well on your course,' Jenna said. 'I should have congratulated you before this. I'm glad for you, and I hope everything goes well for you at the farm.'

She made her escape as soon as she could, going into the office to put her notes from the afternoon onto the computer and hoping that Ross and Annie might have gone by the time she was ready to go home.

She was in luck. The car park was empty when she went out again, and she climbed into the four-wheel drive and headed for the cottage. She didn't want to think about the two of them being together.

Alex came into the surgery next day around lunchtime and caught Jenna as she was writing out repeat prescriptions.

'I'm getting the afternoon ferry and heading for Perth,' he told her, and she put down her pen and studied him.

'Has something happened?' she asked quietly. 'Have you heard from Rebecca?'

'Just a brief little letter. She didn't say very much at all, but I had a phone call from one of her friends who told me in no uncertain terms what a low-life, rotten swine I turned out to be.'

Jenna let out a shocked gasp. 'I can't believe it. Why would she say that?'

He said huskily, 'Because she thinks there's a good chance that Rebecca's pregnant, and that I've abandoned her when she needs me.'

'Oh, no...' She stared up at him in open-mouthed disbelief. 'Didn't you have any idea that might be what was wrong?'

He shook his head. 'It hadn't crossed my mind. I thought she was on the Pill and, anyway, I'd have expected her to tell me straight away if she'd found that she was going to have a baby.'

Jenna bit her lip. 'What are you going to do?'

'I'm going to go over there and tackle her about what's going on,' he said, his voice taking on a fierce note. 'If I'm going to be a father, I've a right to know about it.'

Jenna put her hand on his arm. 'I hope it goes all right. Have you told Ross?'

'No.' He leaned closer and added, 'I don't want him to know. He'll just say I'm an idiot, and think I've behaved irresponsibly. Besides, he has enough on his mind at the moment.'

Her mind clouded with the reminder that Ross was spending all his time with Annie, and she swallowed hard in an attempt to push it away. 'You'll have to tell him something, won't you?'

Footsteps sounded in the doorway, and she glanced quickly around. Ross looked from one to the other, his blue gaze taking in their startled expressions, and he said briskly, 'Is there something going on that I should know about?'

Jenna's lips were suddenly dry and she moistened them carefully with the tip of her tongue. He couldn't have heard what they were saying, could he? She stared at him blankly.

'I know that expression of old,' he said dryly, 'and when I come across the two of you in cahoots like that, it always means trouble.'

Jenna shrugged negligently. 'I can't think why you're saying that.'

'Can't you?' His mouth twisted, and he slanted an assessing gaze over his brother. 'I suppose you have no idea what I'm talking about either?'

'None whatsoever,' Alex said with a bland stare. 'I was just telling Jenna that I'm going over to Perth for a couple of days to meet up with some friends there.'

Ross's dark brow shot upwards. 'That was a sudden decision, wasn't it?'

'Not really. Anyway, I'm going to call in at the hospital on the way and see how Mum's doing. I should be back in time to see her settled back at home.'

Alex left in a little while, and Jenna turned her attention to her prescriptions once more. She tried not to pay any attention to Ross, who was hovering at the edge of her vision, checking notes on the computer.

He came and stood by her a minute or so later, his arm brushing hers as he leaned forward to reach for a slip of paper. She was so conscious of his nearness that her pulse quickened and she felt the heat rising within her to flush her skin with soft colour.

He paused, unmoving for a fraction of time which

prompted her to say, 'Is there something you wanted?'

His shrewd, dark gaze flicked over her, leaving her more confused than ever, but he said simply, 'I thought, if you'd finished here, that we might go over to see how Kirsty's getting on now that she's been discharged from hospital.'

'Has she? Oh, that's good news. Yes, I'd love to see her. It was such a shock finding her like that, and I haven't been able to get it out of my mind ever since.'

They stopped to buy lunch from the bakery in the village, and ate crispy bread rolls and cheese on a park bench by a slow-moving stream where ducks kept a distant eye on them. When they'd finished eating, they threw the remains of their lunch into the water, and watched the birds diving for crumbs.

Ross put an arm around her as they walked back to his car, and even though she realised it was a casual, friendly gesture she felt a gentle glow start up inside her. He murmured softly, 'I shall miss you when you go back to Perth.'

'You could always come and see me over there,' she suggested, trying to keep the huskiness from her voice, not daring to let him see how much she would miss him, too. 'You hardly ever visited when I was working there, and I wondered why. It wasn't for lack of asking.'

She knew the reason, though, didn't she? He had other things on his mind, more important things, and why would he remember a girl who had been such a thorn in his side when she'd lived here?

'You needed to find your feet over there. You'd

been tied to the island for all of your young life, and I didn't think it would be fair to remind you of home when you were getting to grips with a new way of life. Besides, it would have been too difficult to get away, especially when your father was ill, and then afterwards I was on my own a lot of the time, trying to cover the three islands.'

'Things will be different when Dr Bartholomew's here in a couple of weeks, won't they? Once she's found her way around, you'll not be so stretched.'

'I hope so.'

It was just a short journey to Kirsty's home, and when they arrived at the neat little stone-built house, they could hear her childish laughter as she played in the garden at the back.

Kirsty's mother opened the door, her face breaking into a smile when she saw them.

'I shall never forget what you did for her,' she said, clasping Jenna's hands and turning to Ross, who gave her a quick hug. 'We nearly lost her, and I know I couldnae have gone on. I owe you so much.'

She led them out to the garden and they watched Kirsty riding her bike around the paved patio. She stopped pedalling every now and again to shoo the family's dog out of the way or to pick up pebbles from the borders to load into the basket on the front.

The little girl looked up and saw them, then stopped, suddenly shy. Jenna smiled, and Kirsty said, 'You're the lady from the farm, aren't you? I 'meber that, 'cause I showed you the eggs I fetched.' She paused. 'I've been poorly, in 'o'pital.'

'I know you have,' Jenna answered softly. 'How are you feeling, now?'

'A' right. I banged my head.' She pointed to her temple, where there was a thin, red scar. 'See? I banged it there.'

'I can see it. Does it hurt now?'

Kirsty shook her head. 'No.' Then she took off on her bike again down the path, pedalling as fast as her little legs would go.

'I didn't want to let her play on the bike in case she falls over again,' her mother said, 'but she pestered me so, and what can you do?'

'There's no point in wrapping her up in cotton wool, that's for sure,' Ross said. 'The doctors at the hospital were satisfied that she's healthy enough now. Has she suffered any after-effects?'

'No. She seems to be just fine. She doesnae remember much about it, except that she wanted to go after the goats, and then she started to pick some wild flowers. She seems to be more bothered because she lost the flowers when she fell over.'

Ross smiled. 'It's good to see her up and about. If you do have any worries, anything at all, you know where to find me.'

'Aye, I do, Doctor. Thank you for stopping by.'

Ross had some more visits to make, but he dropped Jenna off at the cottage on the way, coming into the house with her for a few minutes.

She gathered up a small pile of post that had landed on her doormat and laid the letters on the table while she went to find some magazines that she'd saved for Flora.

'She'll appreciate these,' he said, rolling them up into a bundle. 'She's uptight because they won't let her out yet, and she's getting restless.'

Jenna would like to have gone with him to visit Flora, but they had to take it in turns so that one could cover for the other. She glanced through the envelopes on the table, and frowned when she saw one that had been franked by the health centre in Perth.

Ross saw her hesitation. 'Is it likely to be news about the job?'

She nodded. 'I can't think of any other reason why they would be writing to me.'

'You'd better open it, then,' he said dryly. 'It's likely to catch fire if you keep staring at it like that.'

She smiled weakly, and tore open the envelope with hands that were more than a little shaky. Taking out the sheet of paper, she scanned the contents briefly, then looked up at Ross.

She just stood there, not saying anything, and he said briskly, 'Well, what do they say? Have you got the job?'

'They want me to start in six weeks' time. I'm to let them have an answer by the end of next week.'

He put his arms around her and pulled her close. Jenna registered the tension in his muscles as he pressured her to him, and she wanted to hold onto him and never let him go.

He kissed her forehead, and she lifted her face so that she could look into his eyes.

'I knew you'd do it,' he said in a roughened tone, and then he lowered his head and gently captured her mouth, his lips brushing lightly over the soft fullness of hers and teasing them apart.

The kiss was endlessly slow and sweet, and it made her long for everything that couldn't be hers. His lips tenderly feathered over her trembling lower lip and swept aside all sense of time and place, until she had no strength left, only a deep-seated desire that made her limbs weaken and turned the warmth in her abdomen to liquid fire.

He dragged his mouth from hers and gazed down at her, his eyes incredibly blue. 'You'll be so good for them,' he murmured huskily. 'You're just the person they need. Well done.'

Right then she didn't feel that it had been well done. It was what she'd worked for, it was what she'd thought she wanted. But instead of feeling any joy in her prize, she felt like weeping, and she wanted to cry out that she wanted it, yes, but what she wanted most of all was him.

Why didn't he need her? Why couldn't she be part of his life?

She didn't say any of those things, though...she couldn't...and when he gently pushed her away from him and left the house, she went and lay down on her bed and wept.

Alex phoned the next day, just after lunch, when she was at the surgery, preparing for a child health clinic. He sounded thoroughly fed up.

'I can't get Rebecca to listen to me,' he complained. 'She told me it's true, she *is* pregnant, but she's insisting that she's going to look after the baby on her own and she doesn't want me around. I don't know how I'm going to get her to see sense, Jen. I can't understand what's gone wrong. She's behaving so oddly.'

'What do you think should happen?'

'I think we should get married. I've told her that's

what we'll do, but she won't listen to me. It's driving me crazy... I just don't know what's going on in her head. I thought she loved me. She said she did, and then everything changed.'

'Perhaps she does—but how is she to know that you really *want* to marry her? Haven't you come up with the idea of marriage because of the baby?'

'Well, of course it's because of the baby.'

She raised a finely arched brow. 'And? Is that the only reason you want to marry her?'

'It's obvious why I want to marry her, isn't it? I love her. Why else would I be tearing my hair out, trying to get her to see sense?'

Jenna said gently, 'Is it obvious? Don't you think you should have another go at explaining your feelings to Rebecca?'

There was silence on the other end of the line, then, 'I'll never understand women. All this stuff about feelings and emotions, as if it isn't all perfectly plain to see. Women! They're a different breed.'

She laughed. 'You're an idiot, Alex. Go and talk to her again.'

She tidied up her table and went to check that everything was in order for the child health clinic that afternoon.

Usually they finished early one day in the week, but the surgeries were getting too busy these days for her to be able to fit the clinics into the morning and she didn't want to leave an extra burden for Laura Bartholomew. She would have enough to do in the first few weeks when she joined the practice.

Ross had been called out to look at a suspected

case of appendicitis, and came back to the surgery to report that it had been a false alarm just as Jenna was seeing her final patient of the day.

She took her pile of notes through to the office, where he was talking to Mairi. He looked tense, she thought, and restless, and she wondered if he'd had another busy evening moving Annie into Flora's house. Perhaps things weren't going as smoothly as he'd hoped.

'How's the move going?' she asked. 'Is Annie settled in now?'

He grimaced. 'We've been moving things around so that she can get some of her own furniture in there, but it hasn't been easy, fitting it all in. Of course, there's a lot of Alex's stuff at the house at the moment.'

'Are you going back there now to do some more?'

'I can't this afternoon. Annie's gone into town to buy some bits and pieces.' He watched as Jenna tidied up the papers in her wire tray and then moved over to the desk. She sat down in front of the computer and typed in a few notes.

He came and leaned against the table, half sitting on the edge of her desk. 'Do you have much more to do?'

'Just about finished,' she said, keying in the last few details. 'Why?'

'Do you fancy a boat ride across the bay? I could do with a bit of fresh air, and there's still some of the afternoon left to enjoy.'

'That sounds like fun. Are you sure there aren't any pressing appointments we should be dealing with?'

'None at all. I cleared the decks this morning so that I could take a break for an hour or two.'

'Wonders will never cease...' She studied him thoughtfully. 'When did you last have a holiday?'

He shrugged. 'I don't remember. Last year some time. I got a bit swamped and there was never a good time.'

'Then we'll definitely take a break now,' she said, frowning.

It was sheer bliss to spend the rest of the afternoon exploring the bay from the deck of the cabin cruiser, with the sun warming her bare arms and the wind gently lifting her hair. Jenna relished it all the more because Ross was with her, his arms guiding her as she took a turn at the wheel, his strong body warm at her back, his cheek almost resting against hers as he leaned forward to point out the rocky shoreline.

'Couldn't you think about having a proper holiday when Dr Bartholomew joins the practice?' she murmured. 'I could stand in for you for a couple of weeks.'

His glance narrowed on her. 'What about the new job?'

'It doesn't start for a few weeks yet, so there would be time for you to fit in a holiday.'

His mouth made an odd grimace. 'I don't think I could do that. It wouldn't be fair to Dr Bartholomew to take off almost as soon as she's started here.'

'I suppose not...' Jenna said slowly. 'I thought maybe we could work something out.'

'I'll think of something. I'll get away one way or another in the summer, so you don't need to get yourself stirred up about it—it's not your problem, Jenna.'

It was a dismissal of sorts, but she wasn't going to let his abrupt tone upset her. It sounded as though he might already have thought of something for later on in the year, and she wondered whether Annie had anything to do with those plans.

She steeled herself not to crumple at the thought. This might be the last afternoon she could share with Ross in carefree enjoyment, and she wanted to make the most of it.

He took over the wheel as they rounded the end of the bay and moved around the far side of the island. There were rocks here, but they stayed clear of them and turned towards a spit of land that stretched some half a mile across.

At low tide, as it was now, it was joined to the island by a stretch of shingle, but when the tide was high the sea would come in and cover this beach. Then the two land masses would be separated by a narrow inlet.

It was beautiful here, but it wasn't visited much by holidaymakers because of the difficulties involved in getting there on foot. For anyone with a boat, though, it was a haven of peace and tranquillity.

Ross carefully brought the boat close to land and moored it at a landing stage, holding a hand out to Jenna when he'd finished to help her down onto the wooden planking.

'Are we all right for the tide?' she asked.

'We should have another hour or so before it starts to come in. Time enough for a quick look around. It won't matter anyway—the boat's secure enough.'

It was lovely there, and it had always been a favourite spot for Jenna. They climbed up to the highest point and looked out over the rolling hills that were all around them, clad in purple heather. Jenna could see a loch in the distance, glittering from the slanting rays of the sun. Nearer to them the land gave way to sheer cliffs and fallen rocks.

As they walked, they saw that there were some people on the beach below them, a family by the look of things. The parents were sitting on a patch of sand, surrounded by towels and bags and their discarded outer clothing, while the children, a boy who looked about twelve years old and a girl some three years younger, were climbing barefoot over the rocks.

The brother and sister were having a great time, laughing and shouting to each other and complaining when the barnacles dug into their feet. The boy was furthest up, showing off to his sister.

'I wonder if they're staying close to here,' Jenna mused. 'Has somebody opened up a campsite while I've been away?'

'Not around here. It's more or less still deserted. They must have trekked some distance and decided to stop and explore for an hour or two.'

Jenna and Ross moved on, climbing down, nearer to the beach so that they could investigate the rock pools, and there the salt tang of seaweed drifted on the air. Jenna wished the day could go on for ever.

The breeze off the sea was cooler now, though, and the sound of the waves breaking on the shore was getting louder. Jenna shivered a little as the sun dipped behind clouds, and Ross put his arm around her to keep her warm.

The family on the beach were getting ready to

leave, and the father was calling out to the children, 'Come down from there now. It's time to go.'

The girl turned around and hopped from one flat rock to another, stopping to collect shells as she went. Then she cried out, and it looked as though she'd hurt her foot. Distressed, she limped back to her mother, who inspected the foot and tried to clean it gently with a tissue.

'It's bleeding,' Jenna heard her say. 'You must have cut it on a shell, Amy. Sit down and hold still and I'll put a towel round it for a minute.'

The man went to fetch his son down from the rocks. The boy looked as though he was uncertain which way to go now that he'd climbed so far. 'Robbie,' his father said, 'come on now. It's time we were getting back.'

As he climbed up higher to guide his son back down, he suddenly missed his footing and slipped and fell onto a jagged edge, twisting his leg as he slithered further down. He shouted out, a harsh cry of pain, and continued falling. It wasn't a long fall, but he landed on a flat rock, writhing in agony.

'That looks like bad news,' Ross said, tensing. 'I'd better go over there and have a look.'

Jenna went with him, picking her way carefully over the rocks until she caught up with him.

'That was a nasty fall,' Ross was saying to the man. 'We're doctors—may we have a look and see what you've done?'

The man nodded, in too much pain to speak just then, his face very pale, and Jenna could see immediately that his ankle was broken. His foot stuck out at an odd angle, and already the tissues surrounding the injured part were beginning to swell.

Ross checked him over to try and discover if he'd hurt himself anywhere else but, apart from some cuts and grazes and a sense of shock, the ankle seemed to have been the worst of it.

Ross tried very gently ease the shoe off the man's foot. The soles of the shoes were smooth, and Jenna thought they might have contributed to the accident, because there was no tread to grip to the rocky surface.

She looked around to see whether the boy had managed to climb down by himself. The last thing they needed now was for another member of the family to be hurt. She was relieved to see that he was standing just a few feet away, safe and sound but looking very frightened by what had happened.

Turning back to Ross, she said in a taut whisper, 'Did you bring a medical bag with you in the boat?'

'Yes, I did,' he answered in an undertone. 'I always carry one with me. But we'll need to splint him somehow and get him back there.'

He spoke quietly to the injured man, who told him his name was David. 'You've fractured your ankle, David, and we'll need to get you to hospital so that you can have it fixed under anaesthetic. I can give you a painkiller once we get you back to my boat, but we need to find something to splint the limb first.'

Jenna went with David's wife to rummage through their scattered belongings to see what they could find, and came back with a cricket bat and a newspaper which they rolled up as best they could. They weren't

ideal, but they would serve to keep the limb reasonably steady and prevent further damage.

'We've a boat moored just a short walk away,'
Jenna told David's wife. 'If we can get you all over
there, we can do a little more to make David more
comfortable and we'll be able to have a better look
at Amy's foot.'

From what she'd seen so far, it wasn't too serious
a wound, but it had bled a lot and would need clean-
ing properly to prevent infection setting in.

Between them they managed to support David,
each putting a shoulder under his armpit and clasping
their hands behind his back. Half lifting, half carrying
him, they helped him across the rough stretch of
beach where already the tide was starting to come in.

Under normal circumstances they would have
climbed to higher ground, but with an injured man
that was an impossibility.

The waves were getting stronger by the minute,
rolling in and breaking around their feet. Jenna's
shoulder and back were aching from the strain, and
she was beginning to long for the sight of the cruiser.
Amy hobbled alongside them with a helping hand
from her mother and brother.

At last they rounded the promontory and came
upon the spit of land near where the boat was moored.
Already the narrow inlet was filling up with sea water,
and soon there would be no chance of walking across.

With an extra burst of energy, they forced their way
across the inlet and made their way to the landing
stage. Stopping there to offload David into a better
position on the wooden decking, they eased him into
the boat and settled him in the small cabin.

It was too cramped in there for all of them to stay, so Ross worked swiftly to open up his medical kit and prepare the injection that would ease David's pain, while Jenna went back onto the landing stage and tended to Amy's foot.

Ross came out of the cabin a short while later and helped the rest of the family on board. Jenna stayed where she was. The boat wasn't built to take more than four or five people, and there was even less room with David stretched out on the seat in the cabin.

'I've alerted the ambulance station,' Ross said, coming over to her on the decking. 'A ferry will be waiting to take him across to the hospital.'

His expression was grave as he looked at Jenna. 'You'll have to take the boat back to the quay, and send someone to pick me up later. Maybe James will come out.'

Jenna shook her head. 'I can't, Ross,' she said in a voice that was almost a whisper. 'The wind's getting up and the sea's too fierce already. I'll never be able to guide the boat around those rocks. It would be too risky, with all those people on board.'

Even Ross would have trouble controlling the craft, judging by the way that the weather conditions were changing. She pressed her lips together to stop them from quivering. 'You'll have to go. You're a better sailor than I am.'

'I can't leave you here. You'll freeze to death.'

'You'll have to, there's no other way. I'll be all right. I'll climb up a bit higher and see if I can find some shelter.' She looked at the craggy slopes all around, and thought she might be able to find a large enough hollow in the cliff wall. 'Go and get David to hospital. Don't worry about me.'

He made a grim little smile. 'That's easy for you to say. It seems to me that I've spent most of my life worrying about you.'

He closed his eyes briefly, thinking hard, but she knew that he recognised what she was saying was right. If she couldn't manage the boat, he had no choice.

'Wait there while I see if I can find something to keep you warm and dry.' He went back on to the boat and disappeared into the cabin for a minute or two. When he came out again he was carrying a sweater and yellow oilskins.

'Put these on,' he ordered. 'They'll at least keep off the worst of the cold.' He looked into her eyes and his gaze was fiercely blue. 'Promise me that you won't take any risks.'

Jenna nodded, and he pointed to large crevice in the headland, fairly near the landing stage. 'Go up there and shelter until I come back for you. You should be protected from the worst of the wind.'

'I will,' she said, and added, more softly, 'Take care.' But Ross was already moving back towards the boat.

CHAPTER NINE

JENNA didn't know how long she had been waiting,
but darkness was falling, and with it the wind was
blowing up to a storm. The roar of the sea below her
as it crashed against the cliff face was a terrifying
sound and she shivered, half with cold and half in
fear.

Sometimes the waves lashed so fiercely and so high
that the salt spray flicked against her face, driven by
the wind. Jenna had never known the water reach as
far up as this deep ledge she was resting on, but quite
often the landing stage would be dashed by the waves.

The oilskins Ross had given her were some pro-
tection against the wind, but even so she huddled
down and wrapped her arms around her knees to
lessen the effects of the cold.

She wished that Ross was here with her. Somehow,
if he had been by her side, she could have borne all
manner of hardships, but without him she felt lost and
afraid.

Would he be safe in the small cabin cruiser? The
journey to the home quay might not be too bad, but
now that the gale was blowing it would be madness
to come back for her. The boat would be no match
for the elements now. It would be broken like match-
wood in these conditions.

She couldn't bear it if anything happened to him.
Tears stung her eyes and she rubbed them away. It

would be best if he stayed away. She could stay here all night if need be, and in the morning, when the weather had settled, someone would come for her.

Then, out of the darkness, Jenna saw a glimmer of a light coming towards her, and her heart gave a strange flip. As the boat drew nearer she realised that it was a large boat, James's probably, a boat built to withstand conditions such as these.

She felt relief that she was being rescued, but there was a kind of sadness in her, too, because, however glad she was to see James right now, it was Ross she wanted to be with most of all.

Jenna started to unwind herself from her huddled shape, getting ready to move down to the landing stage, but a voice called out, 'Stay there,' and a dark figure emerged from the craft and started towards her.

'I'll come and get you down,' the man said again, and though the sound was distorted on the wind, she recognised that it was Ross's voice, and felt a joyous warmth swell up inside her. She could face anything now.

'Hold onto me,' he said, reaching up and putting his arms around her. She clung to him out of sheer relief and he steadied her, before gently supporting her on the slope down to the landing stage. 'Here we go…careful now.'

He helped Jenna down into the rocking boat and drew her into the shelter of the large cabin. Once there, he edged her down onto a seat and sat beside her, hugging her close. James gave her a cheerful grin and gave a thumbs-up sign, before wrestling the boat away from the coast and heading for home.

'I was so afraid that you might have tried to climb

higher up,' Ross muttered, shifting away from her to
delve under a seat and bring out a life jacket.

'Put this on,' he ordered, and when her fingers refused to work properly, he took over. 'Here, let me
help.' He fastened the jacket securely, then sat down
next to her, pulling her against him, his arms going
around her firmly.

'You can't know how desperate I was to get back
to you,' he said huskily. 'I was so scared you
wouldn't be there, that you might have tried something reckless and I would have lost you.'

'But you found me,' Jenna said, her teeth chattering
with the cold, 'and that's all that matters.' Nothing
would ever bother her again if she could have him by
her side. 'I was afraid that you would try to come
back in the cabin cruiser, and you would be broken
up on the rocks. I was imagining the most awful
things—' Her voice broke on a sob. 'I'm just so relieved that you're safe.'

Ross held her tightly for all of the journey home,
as though he didn't dare let her go, and when she
asked about David and his family he said, 'They're
on their way to the hospital. They'll be fine.'

His mouth made a wry shape. 'Though he'll probably need to have metal screws put in to hold the
bones in place, and I expect he'll have his leg in plas-
ter for up to three months. Apart from that, they're in
reasonably good spirits.'

He searched her face quickly. 'Are you still cold?'
She nodded, and his arms fastened around her even
more closely. 'I hated having to leave you there,' he
said thickly, 'but I couldn't see any other way round
it. I called the coastguard, but they had to go on an-

other emergency—a fishing boat that was in trouble further out to sea—and they couldn't get to you straight away. I felt like a desperate man.'

Jenna was astonished that he'd done that. 'I wasn't in any danger,' she protested huskily. 'It was just cold and bleak. I hope you've called them off now that you've found me.'

His mouth curved. 'I will,' he promised, 'when we're safely home.'

It seemed like an age before they were back at the cottage and James was making his way home. Ross bundled Jenna into the sitting room and she took off the oilskins while he built up the fire until there was a good strong blaze.

Then he went and rummaged around upstairs and came back down with sweaters and a duvet, and enveloped Jenna in them until there wasn't a chink showing except for her face.

'I'll make a hot drink,' he said, 'and something to eat. That will help warm you up.' He disappeared again, into the kitchen this time, and she wished that he would hurry up and come back.

'What an end to the day that was.' Ross brought in a tray laden with mugs of mouth-watering hot vegetable soup, crusty rolls and a pot of tea.

Jenna wasn't complaining about the end to the day. She was very content to be snuggled up next to him on the settee while she sipped slowly at her soup.

'Are you warmer now?' he asked, and Jenna nodded, easing the duvet away from herself. 'Good. Are you feeling up to talking seriously? There's something I need to say to you.'

She nodded, her brows drawing together in a small

frown. 'What's it about? Is something wrong?' Then a horrifying thought struck her and she said with a shocked gasp, 'It's not your mother, is it? Nothing's happened to Flora?'

'No, nothing like that. She's doing fine, she'll be coming home tomorrow.'

Jenna sank back in relief. 'Oh, thank heaven for that. You had me worried there for a minute.'

'The thing is,' Ross said, 'I want to ask you about something. I know this is the wrong time to be loading you with problems, but it's fairly urgent and I can't put it off. It's to do with work—and you need to think about it carefully.'

He was watching her closely, making sure that she was following him.

'Have I done something wrong?' She didn't recall making any mistakes, but perhaps she'd filled in the wrong form for something.

'No, of course not,' he said. 'It's about the job at the paediatric centre... I know that it's what you had set your heart on, but I wondered if you were up to considering something else?'

Jenna looked at him blankly, and he went on swiftly, 'I've been thinking about starting up a centre here on the island to provide obstetric and child health clinics. The way things are now, it would be too much for either myself or Dr Bartholomew to handle, and I can't think of anyone better equipped to run it than you. What do you think about it?'

His suggestion startled her so much that she couldn't answer him straight away. She simply stared at him, her green eyes very wide, and Ross went on quickly, 'It's been on my mind to ask you for some

time now, but I always hesitated because of my promise to your father to support you in what you wanted
to do. I know that he thought you had set your heart
on working in a big medical centre where you could
specialise...but I can't help thinking that you should
at least look at other opportunities.'

'You mean he might have thought the centre that
you're planning might not be a large enough propo-
sition?'

'That's right. It won't be anything like a city paediatric centre. But I do know that you love this island...and I think that might compensate for what you
would lose in other ways. I think you might be happy
working here. Will you at least think about it?'

Jenna was stunned by what he was saying, and she
needed to be very sure that this wasn't all just a fig-
ment of her imagination.

'Will you be able to set it up, just like that?' she
asked him carefully. 'Won't it take a lot of funding?'

'It will take a fair amount of funding, yes. But this
isn't something I've come up with out of the blue. A
few years ago the population here was dwindling as
people moved away, but that seems to be changing
now. A growing number of holidaymakers have come
here, taken a shine to the place and decided that they
wanted to stay. And the birth rate has been rising here
over the last year or so, and we need to take account
of that.'

Ross reached for her hand and clasped it in his.
'We're going to need someone who can deal with
problems specific to children, and you're the best person I can think of to do that, Jenna. I wanted to ask
you before, but it's taken me all this time to find

sponsors and arrange funding with the bank for an extension to the surgery.'

He stopped talking and looked at her intently, searching her face for any sign that she was considering it.

'You've taken me completely by surprise,' she said. 'I wasn't expecting anything like this.'

'I know it isn't anything like the promotion that you've been offered,' he said seriously, 'and you would have to work in fairly cramped conditions at the surgery until the new extension is up and running...but will you at least think about it? You won't turn it down out of hand?'

She felt as though her head were spinning. 'Of course I'll think about it... I just need—'

Jenna broke off as the phone started to ring, and she jumped, startled by the intrusion. 'I hope that's not an emergency call-out.' The last thing she wanted now was for either one of them to have to go out. Then she realised that if it had been a patient, it would have been Ross's phone that was ringing.

It was Alex. 'Good news,' he said, and she could tell from his voice that he was brimming over with cheerfulness.

'Why? What's going on?' She mouthed Alex's name to Ross, and watched his jaw clench. She marvelled at how he managed to look impatient and frustrated all at the same time. He got to his feet and started pacing the room.

'Like you said,' Alex explained, 'she thought I was telling her I would marry her just because of the baby. She didn't think I really wanted to take on a wife and family because I've always been happy-go-lucky, and

I'm still a student with exams to take before I can think about getting a job.'

'She has a point there, don't you think?'

'Of course she has. It's going to be difficult, and we're going to find it hard to manage for a while. We have to find somewhere to live, for one thing. Rebecca's still with her parents.'

'Have you made any plans?'

'Only insofar as I need to get my qualification and find a job. They're my priorities right now. I couldn't get down to the studying before because I was worried about what was going on with Rebecca and me...but I feel more settled now. I know that it's all going to work out in the end.'

'Will there be a problem with finding a job?'

'I don't think so. There's a place coming up at the veterinary practice on the island—I spoke to Ray MacPherson about it and he said that if my results were good he'd give me a chance.'

'That sounds really good. I'm glad for you, Alex. Do you want a word with Ross? He's here with me now.'

Jenna handed the phone to Ross, and from what she could gather their conversation was mostly about Flora and her homecoming the following day.

Ross cut the call a few minutes later, looking thoroughly perplexed. 'He reckons he's coming home to get down to some serious studying. What's all that about?'

'Didn't he say?'

He shook his head, then said dryly, 'Perhaps he's feverish. Do you know what's going on?'

'I think I do, but I'd rather Alex told you himself.'

Ross looked at her closely, his expression grim. 'Is this anything to do with you and Alex?'

'Alex and me?' Jenna smiled at the notion. 'I tried to explain to you about Alex and me once before, but you wouldn't believe me. I love him dearly—but like a brother. We've always been close, we practically grew up together, so it's hardly surprising, is it?'

He was still watching her doubtfully. 'You always had a crush on him.'

'Not in the way you think. We've shared so much all our lives. Anyway, I think you'll find that he's moving on to other things now. You'll have to talk to him about that when he comes home. I can't speak for him—he must do that himself.'

She wished Ross would stop pacing so that she could think more clearly. 'Tell me some more about this job,' she said. 'You've given me a lot to think about, just when I thought everything was done and dusted. Does Dr Bartholomew know about it? After all, it will affect her in some way because she might have been expecting to cover the paediatric side of things herself.'

'She'll have enough to do, covering the daily surgeries and home visits, and she wants to have a say in running a call-in centre for the holidaymakers. In the holiday season the extra numbers can play havoc with day-to-day surgeries. If you were to take on the mother-and-baby side of things and child health assessments and follow-up clinics, that would ease the burden on the practice tremendously. Will you think about it—or are you committed to going to the mainland?'

Jenna said carefully, 'I went to the mainland originally because I wanted to study medicine and follow in my father's footsteps…and because I stayed there everyone assumed that was what I wanted. I tried to convince myself that it was what I'd always worked for.'

She gave an odd little grimace. 'There was no way I could come back here and work alongside you and my father. There was no place for me—or so I thought. Being on the mainland wasn't a choice for me—it was the only thing I could do.'

He pulled in a breath, his brows meeting in a thick, dark line. 'Are you saying that you'll take the job?'

'Oh, yes,' she said softly. 'I want to take this job more than anything.'

His mouth curved in a wide smile. Then he let out a whoop of triumph, and came over to grab her by the waist and swing her around in sheer exhilaration. 'Brilliant. That's wonderful, Jenna. I'm really glad you said yes.'

Reluctantly, Ross put her down a moment later, steadying her as she slid down his long body. His powerful thighs nudged hers, her breasts were softly crushed against his firm chest and her senses swam with the joy of simply having him near.

At the back of her mind, though, there was a niggling doubt as to whether she was doing the right thing in staying on here. Wasn't she bringing more ultimate heartache down on herself? How could she work with him each and every day, knowing that in the end he would be going home to Annie?

While she was in his firm embrace it was so hard to think clearly. She looked up at him, her green gaze taking in the strongly sculpted lines of his dear face, the firm, beautifully moulded curve of his mouth, and she longed for him to reach down and touch his lips to hers.

Her glance meshed with his and, as though he'd read her thoughts, he bent his head and kissed her, a sweet, endlessly heart-wrenching kiss that plundered the depths of her being.

When he finally dragged his lips from hers, he said huskily, 'I want more than just to have you stay here and work with me, Jenna—don't you know that? I want to have you with me at all times, to share everything in our lives together…and I mean everything. Most of all, I want to have you wake up beside me every morning. Am I hoping for too much?'

Confused, she said falteringly, 'But you and Annie… Alex thought that you were planning a June wedding…'

His blue eyes danced with amusement. 'How could we possibly do that when I'm in love with you?'

'Are you?' she asked breathlessly, her eyes widening.

'Didn't you know that already? Surely you did? Haven't I shown you in a thousand ways how much you mean to me?'

His thumb gently traced the line of her cheek. 'Annie is a friend, a very dear friend, who is a thoroughly capable young woman and exactly the right person to be taking care of my mother.'

'But you and she… You used to date each other…you were always together, even years ago when I left to do my training.'

'We went around together, but it was never serious.

And, anyway, Annie has a boyfriend already. He works away a lot of the time on the oil rigs.'

'But Alex thought—'

'What does Alex know about anything?' Ross's hands curved around her arms. 'You know, where Alex is concerned, my feelings have been so mixed up. He's my brother, but when I thought you wanted him I couldn't handle it at all. I felt anger and frustration raging inside me, and I didn't know how to cope with any of it.'

He put a hand under her chin and tilted her face up to him. 'I love you, Jenna. I think I've loved you for all of my life...and sometimes I think it's more than I can bear to have you leave me, even for a day. When I had to leave you on that landing stage, I vowed I would move heaven and earth to keep you in my life. I never want to be apart from you again.'

Jenna smiled up at him, a watery smile because a sheen of tears was blurring her vision. 'I think,' she whispered, 'that you might have just made me the happiest woman on earth.'

'Does that mean that you love me, too?'

'With all my heart,' she said huskily.

Ross kissed her again, and she clung to him, not wanting their lips to part, wanting the ecstasy of this moment to go on for ever.

After an eternity he muttered raggedly against her mouth, 'Will you marry me? Will you be mine, and be with me for all time?'

'Oh, yes,' she murmured, losing herself in the perfect magic of his embrace. 'For all time.'

MILLS & BOON®

Makes any time special™

JANUARY 2001 HARDBACK TITLES

ROMANCE™

The Demetrios Virgin *Penny Jordan*   H5348 0 263 16948 0
To Become A Bride *Carole Mortimer*   H5349 0 263 16949 9
The Irresistible Tycoon *Helen Brooks*   H5350 0 263 16950 2
The Unlikely Mistress *Sharon Kendrick*   H5351 0 263 16951 0
A Vengeful Deception *Lee Wilkinson*   H5352 0 263 16952 9
Morgan's Secret Son *Sara Wood*   H5353 0 263 16953 7
Expecting His Baby *Sandra Field*   H5354 0 263 16954 5
The Twenty-Four-Hour Groom *Laura Anthony*
                                                  H5355 0 263 16955 3
His Runaway Bride *Liz Fielding*   H5356 0 263 16956 1
The Substitute Wife *Barbara McMahon*   H5357 0 263 16957 X
Accidental Fiancée *Renee Roszel*   H5358 0 263 16958 8
The Motherhood Campaign *Heather MacAllister*
                                                  H5359 0 263 16959 6
Babies and a Blue-Eyed Man *Myrna Mackenzie*
                                                  H5360 0 263 16960 X
The Irresistible Prince *Lisa Kaye Laurel*   H5361 0 263 16961 8
Practising Partners *Joanna Neil*   H5362 0 263 16962 6
A Father For Her Child *Barbara Hart*   H5363 0 263 16963 4

HISTORICAL ROMANCE™

Rosalyn and the Scoundrel *Anne Herries*   H495   0 263 16924 3
Carnival Of Love *Helen Dickson*   H496   0 263 16925 1

MEDICAL ROMANCE™

Doctor on Loan *Marion Lennox*   M413   0 263 16900 6
A Nurse in Crisis *Lilian Darcy*   M414   0 263 16901 4

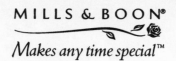

MILLS & BOON®

Makes any time special™

JANUARY 2001 LARGE PRINT TITLES

ROMANCE™

The Marriage Deal *Helen Bianchin*	1351	0 263 16732 1
Mistress on Loan *Sara Craven*	1352	0 263 16733 X
For the Sake of His Child *Lucy Gordon*	1353	0 263 16734 8
Innocent Sins *Anne Mather*	1354	0 263 16735 6
The Italian's Revenge *Michelle Reid*	1355	0 263 16736 4
Passion's Baby *Catherine Spencer*	1356	0 263 16737 2
Rafael's Love-Child *Kate Walker*	1357	0 263 16738 0
The Billionaire and the Baby *Rebecca Winters*		
	1358	0 263 16739 9

HISTORICAL ROMANCE™

The Youngest Dowager *Francesca Shaw*	0 263 16888 3
A Strange Likeness *Paula Marshall*	0 263 16889 1

MEDICAL ROMANCE™

Doctors at Odds *Drusilla Douglas*	0 263 16820 4
Heart at Risk *Helen Shelton*	0 263 16821 2
Greater Than Riches *Jennifer Taylor*	0 263 16822 0
Marry Me *Meredith Webber*	0 263 16823 9

MILLS & BOON®

Makes any time special™

FEBRUARY 2001 HARDBACK TITLES

ROMANCE™

The Arabian Mistress *Lynne Graham*	H5364	0 263 16964 2
A Sicilian Seduction *Michelle Reid*	H5365	0 263 16965 0
Marriage At A Price *Miranda Lee*	H5366	0 263 16966 9
Husband For Real *Catherine George*	H5367	0 263 16967 7
Claiming His Wife *Diana Hamilton*	H5368	0 263 16968 5
The Boss's Proposal *Cathy Williams*	H5369	0 263 16969 3
A Ruthless Passion *Robyn Donald*	H5370	0 263 16970 7
The Prince's Heir *Sally Carleen*	H5371	0 263 16971 5
The Marriage Project *Day Leclaire*	H5372	0 263 16972 3
A Suitable Husband *Jessica Steele*	H5373	0 263 16973 1
A Convenient Affair *Leigh Michaels*	H5374	0 263 16974 X
A Bride for Barra Creek *Jessica Hart*	H5375	0 263 16975 8
Prim, Proper…Pregnant *Alice Sharpe*	H5376	0 263 16976 6
Emma and the Earl *Elizabeth Harbison*	H5377	0 263 16977 4
The Midwife's Child *Sarah Morgan*	H5378	0 263 16978 2
Sara's Secret *Anne Herries*		H5379 0 263 16979 0

HISTORICAL ROMANCE™

A Roguish Gentleman *Mary Brendan*	H497	0 263 16926 X
The Westmere Legacy *Mary Nichols*	H498	0 263 16927 8

MEDICAL ROMANCE™

Rescuing Dr Ryan *Caroline Anderson*	M415	0 263 16902 2
Found: One Husband *Meredith Webber*	M416	0 263 16903 0

MILLS & BOON®

Makes any time special™

FEBRUARY 2001 LARGE PRINT TITLES

ROMANCE™

The Husband Assignment *Helen Bianchin*	1359	0 263 16740 2
The Bride's Proposition *Day Leclaire*	1360	0 263 16741 0
The Playboy's Virgin *Miranda Lee*	1361	0 263 16742 9
Mistress of the Sheikh *Sandra Marton*	1362	0 263 16743 7
Rhys's Redemption *Anne McAllister*	1363	0 263 16744 5
Georgia's Groom *Barbara McMahon*	1364	0 263 16745 3
Secret Seduction *Susan Napier*	1365	0 263 16746 1
Marriage in Mind *Jessica Steele*	1366	0 263 16747 X

HISTORICAL ROMANCE™

Knight's Move *Jennifer Landsbert*	0 263 16890 5
An Innocent Deceit *Gail Whitiker*	0 263 16891 3

MEDICAL ROMANCE™

Nurse Friday *Margaret O'Neill*	0 263 16824 7
A Man To Be Trusted *Gill Sanderson*	0 263 16825 5
Prescriptions and Promises *Jessica Matthews*	0 263 16826 3
Danger - Dr Heartbreak *Elisabeth Scott*	0 263 16827 1